You don't find love, it finds you.
It's got a little bit to do with kismet,
one's destiny and fate,
and what's written in the stars.
~ Anais Nin

Love doesn't meet you at your best.
It meets you in your mess.
~ J.S. Park

Don't find love, let love find you.
That's why it's called falling in love.
Because you don't force yourself to fall,
you just fall.

Love isn't something you find.
Love is something that finds you.
~ Loretta Young

Your flaws are perfect,
for the heart that is meant to love you.
~ Trent Shelton

True love should not have to lie, cheat, or
steal. The best kind of love finds you
when you need it most.
~ Shelly Crane

The heart has its reasons which
reason knows nothing of…
We know the truth not only by the reason,
but by the heart.
~ Blaise Pascal

When I saw you, I fell in love, and
you smiled because you knew.
~ William Shakespeare

Love has reasons
which reason cannot understand.
~ Sanz Edwards

Amor vincit omnia. Love conquers all.
~ Latin

Something just like this.
~ The Chainsmokers & Coldplay

If you search for relationships,
you will never end up in the right one.
Let love find you.
Let him go. If he returns, he's yours.
If he doesn't, he was never meant to be.

A Kismet Romance Book One

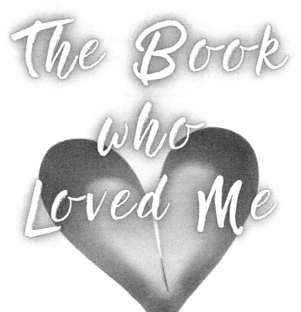

The Book who Loved Me

**Crossing Time
Connecting Soul Mates**

SANZ EDWARDS

Edited by John Sutton

Words are the only true magic. Names, characters, places, and incidents are either the product of the author's imagination or used fictitiously.

Follow the author on Instagram: @sanz_edwards
Support the continued creation of this series on Patreon.
See the next books develop with weekly updates and excerpts on: https://www.patreon.com/sanz_edwards

ISBN (hardcover)
ISBN (paperback) 979-8-78-370541-0
ISBN (ebook)
[Love. Romance. Soul Mates. Kismet. Fate. Destiny. Second-chances. Self-love. Self-Discovery. Families. Divorce. Death. Forgiveness. Travel.]

Printed in the United States of America.

First Edition
12.2021
Updated Edition
3.2022

For my kids, Dain & Shalee –

You are the loves of my life.
I hope you find the kind of deep, abiding love
that fills and completes you.

For Mom –

Thank you for river rafting in your 60s,
and teaching me it is never too late
(and that some of us are just late bloomers).

For my love –

Thank you for loving me and
showing me how it felt to be loved unconditionally,
even when I didn't and couldn't love myself.
And teaching me how easily it can be lost if it
isn't taken care of and cherished.

Contents

Chapter 1 1

Chapter 2 17

Chapter 3 31

Chapter 4 36

Chapter 5 43

Chapter 6 51

Chapter 7 58

Chapter 8 68

Chapter 9 87

Chapter 10 96

Chapter 11 99

Chapter 12 117

Chapter 13 124

Chapter 14 130

Chapter 15 146

Chapter 16 155

Chapter 17 172

Bonus Content 183

A Note from the Author 185

How This Book Came to Be 188

What to Expect in:

The Book who Knew Me 193

The Book
who
Loved Me

Chapter 1

Esmae was just peculiar enough that having an inner Irish male voice narrate events in third person caused her no concern, at first. As she walked along a dirt path lined by thick trees on one side and the sparkling water of Detroit Lake on the other, she found the short bursts of description rather comforting and bemusingly insightful. *...The sun streamed through trees as it would through the same sort of trees, well like, anywhere in the world on a sunny day like today....In the distance, a small child slipped as he threw stones, his mother saved him from falling. The ungrateful, snippet of a child was having none of it and pulled away from her grasp. Slipping and being saved, again, by his lovin' mam.... The haunting coo of a collared dove echoed a place of missing bygone memories and loving wants.*

A collared dove? Esmae wondered why her inner narrator would say collared dove when it was a mourning dove, her favorite bird. Well, favorite next to the coo of a Minnesota loon. Both birds mated for life, with a bond so strong they watched over their deceased mate and tried to care for them. The thought made her heart ache and her eyes teared up.

Not today, she decided.

Esmae brushed aside the tear and any other dove questions. This was just her inner monologue trying out this new voice—again, after eight months of silence. Yes, a little unusual one of her inner voices was male. Stranger, and most unexpected, was how perfect the Irish accent seemed. The only Irish accent she knew was from her grandfather, who used a broken Irish-English accent to be silly and tease her, and from Pierce Brosnan in *Remington Steele*, where his accent could not possibly be considered true Irish. Still, this narrator with his strong Irish accent only caused concern and a deep unsettling feeling when Esmae reached her destination and he started to narrate her movements. Esmae never narrated her actions, not like this, not in this detail.

She felt the smooth, worn brass on the knob and heard the harmonious twinkle of the bell at odds with the creak of the hinge as she pushed open the door to Lady Myrtle's Shoppe of Oddities, Curiosities, & Books. She stepped within this quaint shoppe full of old-fashion charm, closed her eyes, and inhaled…deeply. The must from stacks of old, worn books mingled with the odds and ends. Ye, an aroma only a true lover of books and things weird and wonderful would, or could, appreciate and yearn for.

Part used books and part thrift store, this was a place where the curious could get lost for days exploring the multiple shelves and deep nooks layered with asthores, the endearments of the heart. This was a place where organization could not be detected by any mere passerby or interloper. The subtle, perfectly imperfect organization was reserved for the intuitive remembrance of the one and only Lady Myrtle…and the small signs posted around the shoppe.

Lady Myrtle and her husband, Lord Earl, were not by title Lord and Lady. But somewhere by blood they were related to some Lord, as a sordid tale handed down from generation to generation. They had genealogy papers somewhere proving this connection, but that was the only thing Myrtle couldn't find after five decades of owning the shop. If any other particular or peculiar item was desired, she would know if she had it and the general area in which to find it. Might be at the bottom of a few oddities, a spackle of curiosities, and a ton of books, but the search was worth the treasure and a few others gathered along the quest.

This wasn't the first time Esmae had the unsettling feeling of being watched, then brushed it aside. No one could telepathically send these narrative thoughts into her head. She didn't know what to do beyond acceptance of the voice and that she wasn't going crazy, because, despite the strangeness of a deep, manly voice being verbally intimate, she felt goosebumps rise on her arms and long forgotten twinkles in other places. This made his voice and presence in her life real; he was a part of her and his surprising accuracy soothed her.

For over two years, this inner Irish voice appeared unexpectedly. At first, he narrated a few small, insignificant moments like a rainy day which produced a double rainbow, the sun setting and the pink wisps turning into dark cordial cherries, two lovers walking the boardwalk alongside the lake and stopping to kiss, observing the uniqueness of strangers as they passed, and even the views she enjoyed as she rode a bike around the lake her family had called home for four generations.

These scenes in her life described what she saw and experienced, not about her. Even the pensive, hesitant narration present for a few mournful and heartbreaking moments of Esmae's life, hadn't been about her but what she saw happening and observed.

Because of her inner male voice's narration, she hadn't felt alone when her grandfather died last year. However weird and peculiar, however strange and uncanny, even if it was her imagination, even if others might think she was a bit crazy to think this voice was a connection to someone beyond her, this someone, this Irish someone, made her feel she wasn't alone, that someone understood the depth of loss she felt at losing her last parental figure, her grandfather, her guardian since her parents had died when she was five.

His Irish presence, even as a voice in her head, added poignancy, insight, a little humor, and, dare she admit, comfort. When her grandpa died, the narrator, usually light and upbeat, spoke with somber and delicate reverence of the funeral, the procession, and the wake.

Well, somber until he humorously drew Esmae's attention — or she drew her own attention, she wasn't quite sure — to a line of five of her youngest cousins, ages three to six, slipping cake from the table at the wake, then rounding through the kitchen and living room to come back to slip off two more each, having stuffed the other pieces in their mouths. Their faces smeared with chocolate frosting and covered with crumbs. *Aw, to be that young and be unconcerned about death*, the voice yearned. Esmae yearned with him.

Later that night, the inner voice was with her and a large group of friends and family by the firepit in the backyard with the waves of Long Lake lapping on shore — her grandpa's favorite spot. They all joined in with an earnest rendition of "Danny Boy."

She mouthed the words as she listened to her Irish narrator sing it the way it was meant to be and the way her English grandpa "and a wee bit Irish", as he would say, sang it himself late at night when he thought no one was listening. The rest of the night the voice was silent. Esmae imagined they spent it together listening to the many stories and toasts.

The most intimate moment, the one she wished hadn't

been narrated, was when she found out last Valentine's Day her husband of twenty-five years had been cheating on her, not only once but numerous times, and was in love with someone else. Thirty-two years of being together fell apart. The ache in her heart, the sick feeling in the pit of her stomach, she thought life was over. Her inner narrator knew better. *She thought she would never love again. She thought she would become a spinster living her days alone…with cats. She was wrong.*

Esmae knew she heard care and empathy in his inflection, like he, too, understood the pain of lost love. Relief washed over her as she trusted her inner voice. The stress of not being loved and maybe never finding love again, of not ever being good enough to be picked, evaporated like dew in the morning.

At least, for a little while.

His narration flickered into her life, a flame burning for a few sentences or a few paragraphs or longer like that one night, then flickering out. During the last eight months, she tried conjuring the Irish voice up on her own, but could never do it. The narrator presented himself when he wanted. Almost like a ghost or spirit, she mused.

Esmae thought about him when he wasn't around with his wry humor, especially when dealing with her separation, finding a place to live, and turning forty-seven without a celebration, without love, and without having close family around. She wondered where the inner Irish voice disappeared to and why she couldn't make him appear when she wanted.

With a peculiar, crooked smile, Esmae accepted there was nothing she could do about the voice as he continued… *She took two more steps into the shop, sang out "Lady Myrtle" as lyrics for the door and bell's closing cacophony.*

Esmae jumped as from nowhere Myrtle's hand gently and unexpectedly touched Esmae's arm. "Oh, honey," Myrtle chuckled. "So sorry. Were you deep in thought? Or daydreaming about that handsome voice in your head?"

Only Myrtle would think a voice in her head could be described as "handsome". Of course, she did think the voice was handsome, too. Esmae's cheeks flushed as she chuckled a little embarrassed, and smiled at Myrtle, whose soft grey eyes twinkled with mischief. She understood, like no one else, that Esmae wasn't crazy, even though they both thought she was crazy when the voice first appeared. Others had, too. Now, Myrtle was the only one she talked to about him. To the rest of the world — her therapist, lawyer, kids, and almost ex, she told them she didn't hear his voice anymore and that it must have been her mind playing tricks, projecting her desire to travel to Ireland.

But Myrtle thought an Irish voice in anyone's head was the most romantic occurrence, ripe with destiny. Anything was possible when it was meant to be.

"What I wouldn't do for a ....," Myrtle sighed and squeezed Esmae's arm knowingly. Life's experiences had weathered her with age and wrinkles, bones and veins showed distinctly through her thin skin, but she exuded a welcoming warmth which radiated like rose gold from her cheeks and filled the space around her, making her seem ten times her stature. This kind essence surrounded and embraced all who came within a few feet of her.

"I miss my Lord Earl." She fingered a locket at her neck and smiled a sad, knowing smile. Then, with brightness, said, "Staying for tea?" Myrtle looked at the package Esmae held. "Did you bring some more?"

Esmae handed her a package with a couple jars of peach brandy jam and ten plastic wrapped packages of her famous candied, pumpkin spiced walnuts and pecans.

"These make my mouth water just thinking about them," Myrtle licked her bottom lips daintily. Then smacked them together. "I promise we'll sell most of them. This time." She winked at Esmae. Taking two of the packages, she handed the rest back to Esmae. "Here, put the rest at the checkout counter, or I may not be able to stop." Myrtle chuckled and turned to the kitchen without waiting for an answer. "I'll put a pot on."

Esmae watched the energetic sprite almost float her way on the worn path through a dense forest of overgrown stacks. It was hard to imagine Myrtle ever over-indulging in a candied nut, like Esmae had last night while she made them. Ten packages had been fifteen.

"Thanks, Myrtle," Esmae followed on the same path, through the porch entrance, and stepped toward the counter. "You remember I work tonight, right?"

"Oh, yes, dear," Myrtle's voice echoed from the back, the clack of the teapot on the stove and the teacups on the counter accompanying Myrtle's sweetness.

Esmae knew she didn't have to wonder what teacup Myrtle would choose for her, it was always the same one. There was a whole room full of teacups with names on the bottom along with the day they had their first tea with Myrtle. The tearoom, especially built as an addition to the kitchen by Lord Earl, held hundreds of unique teacups, one for each person who had wandered in and stayed for tea. They had a permanent place and no one ever doubted which cup was theirs. Esmae thought of the large ceramic mug with waves of blue paint and a turquoise stone embedded on its question mark-twirled handle. Myrtle had presented Esmae with this when her grandmother died. The waves represented her love of the lakes and the turquoise stone was her grandma's favorite jewel. Now the cup reminded her of both her grandparents and parents, and the black tea reminded her of the English black tea her great-grandma used to make.

Esmae sighed with reminiscence and how quickly time passes and life changes. After placing the candied nuts on the counter by the checkout register, she turned to survey the shoppe. There was a cart of books somewhere with additional odds and ends of curiosities waiting for her to put away.

Esmae unconsciously touched the books stacked on the shelves and the Irish narrator continued...*as she lightly fingered the books, some with enough dust her fingers left etchings.* Esmae made a mental note to dust those later. *There were smooth covers, some with texture, corners with ragged edges with threads loose. Turning a corner, her attention was diverted by prisms hanging from a lamp. The triangular, transparent crystals dripped into points. She gently flipped one and rays reflected a pointed light of brightness across her face and illuminated down another aisle.*

Esmae wondered if the narrator enjoyed these explorations as much as she did. These adventures satiated a deep part of her, the gypsy wanderer in her. Did he realize this was the only way this part of her could be satiated? There was no way to be sure what motivated the narrator and if he knew her motives.

The plethora of items waited for an acknowledging caress, for they knew her. To her, they seemed alive, and they wished she could take them all home. What tales they would tell when she read them. If they could talk, what stories the other items might divulge of their journey to Lady Myrtle's Shoppe. She imagined the harrowing peril of almost being thrown away before being rescued and placed in Myrtle's care.

Esmae smiled. He knew her and how she imagined each item having a personality and a sordid tale of woe. Because, only cast offs found their way to Myrtle's, like she had in her most dismal and depressing time. This was Lady Myrtle's speciality, knowing when someone or something needed a place of rescue.

Her Irish narrator accompanied Esmae as she continued to roam around the shoppe, loving each piece, filling herself with the deep enjoyment of caring for these treasures and imagining their tales, using them as unwritten fables she pretended to write for her own entertainment. She had made up stories for her children as she put them to bed years ago, before they were grown and didn't need her stories anymore.

Only the narrator seemed to understand her imagination and the life of each piece, interjecting bits and pieces of his own fanciful perception.

Books haphazardly covered the shelves of bookcases made of oak, maple, some painted black or white. They were generously stacked in front of *those longing to be read and on top of others, who believed they already had a home there in the shoppe. Some hiding, not wanting to leave, waiting for the right moment to be found.* Stacked solidly on top of the tall shelves, stuffed sideways in the nooks, and on piles started on the floor stood as tall as a toddler, in corners, anyway they fit, *the well-read books tattered and worn with experience, young books with no dogears waiting patiently to share their wisdom. The shelves held these books together as family.*

No organization existed except for the section names placed on the sides of the bookcases. The eclectic collection of books and bookcases began small and grew as more people donated or Myrtle and Earl found them at auction sales. "They seem to call to me to give them a home," Myrtle said one day as they were dusting, then getting lost in the found but forgotten treasures. There were plenty of sales, but *the space quickly filled as more of the lost were found and the strange and wonderful accepted.*

At the front and sides of the shop, glass cases and other eccentric storages like old luggage, trunks, and ornament wrought-iron tables showcased the oddities and curiosities. Two stuffed cats, one black and one white, stood guard across from each other at end of two glass cases. Their green eyes following customers as they entered. Beneath their feet, the glass cases were filled with weirdness like a baby holding a vase and a ceramic melted snowman made by Carol Sue, its hat, corncob pipe, twigs for arms, and eyes of coal sticking out from melting balls of snow, and a pool of water formed underneath.

Trinkets such as an 1800s wooden penny, a locket from a war bride still held pictures of the couple blurred by salty teardrops—*he never came back, his last thoughts of her*, a round piece of glass held a mustard seed of faith, a rabbit's foot for good luck—*how lucky is a rabbit who lost his foot*, an eye of newt—which was a green glass marble with a brown spot at its center, tarot cards, amulets, anything anyone possibly wanted.

At the checkout counter, Myrtle had positioned an antique ceramic blue genie rising out of an Arabian oil lamp with billowing smoke. When a penny was offered, Myrtle pushed a button behind the genie, and he bowed and lowered his arms at the same time. After the wish was made, the penny was placed in his hand. The weight of the penny made the genie raise his body, his arms going over his head and the penny disappeared into his turban and slid into the bottle, which played an exotic tune.

There was no guarantee the wish of lost love, found keys, a trip to Europe, or a puppy would come true instantly, but if the wisher wanted a certain book or other oddity or curiosity, the genie might help the shop provide it. At the very least, it would have a possibility of happening…and it usually happened within a week to a few months, if Myrtle had any say about it.

If a person, old or young, came in for love, Myrtle always readied a cuppa tea and a chat by the fire. That alone worked the magic, especially since each person signed the teacup with their name and the date, then placed it in the tearoom *so they always knew they were never forgotten and always welcomed.* More than any genie in a lamp, this allowed the heart to heal and be given hope. Even when people wished for what they wanted rather than for what they needed, the teacup was a remedy for all things. Esmae couldn't even begin to count the number of cups and pots of tea Myrtle had made, much less drank, since the shop opened in 1950.

A few days ago, Esmae walked in on a young teen drying her tears after tea with Myrtle. Then, when Myrtle hugged the teen close, she didn't pat. A solid hug for five minutes, and the girl left with more confidence and less of a broken heart.

The uncanny intuition of Lady Myrtle, Esmae and her inner voice thought at the same time.

Another of Esme's favorite spots was the huge stone fireplace with a couch on the left and two highbacked chairs with a small table in between. On the right of the chairs, in the corner of the built-in shelves alongside the fireplace, stood a wooden carved tree the same height as Esmae. The tree's wooden branches stretched out offering leaves of wood which Myrtle used to display birds, a few exotic stuffed birds, different sizes and colors of glass birds, a few with straw nests, and one prehistoric bird with reptilian teeth stood at its trunk — the dangerous eyes and sharp teeth either made children cry or they placed the other birds on display in its beak as though the carnivorous bird was eating a feathery meal.

Hanging near the top of the tree were two turtle doves which fit together in a heart-shaped ornament. Next to this was Esmae's favorite, an ornament of two loons floating on a blue glass lake with three babies trailing behind, forever together.

Prisms of all shapes and sizes also hung from the tree and throughout the shoppe in the windows, on the outside of some bookcases and hung like rain drops from the porch ceiling to greet those who entered when they opened the door. They reflected the light and pierced the shadows during the day. Some hung with tiny scars or cracks and *some still looked for their purpose.*

Turn after turn...others would have lost their way. The further back a person travelled into the shoppe was like stepping back in time. The distinct old book smell of almond, vanilla, and grass beckoned the curious, the lonely, the ones looking for comfort, and the ones destined for more.

"Myrtle," Esmae said so Myrtle could hear through the stacks, "is there anything new?"

"Go to the end of the row. Turn left then right, toward me, dear," Myrtle's perception continued to surprise Esmae.

What Inis didn't know was Myrtle wanted to add, "There is something destined for you around the corner" but didn't.

Esmae's heart skipped a beat in anticipation. And in the same instance was confused, who the heck was Inis?

Chapter 2

"Oh, look. It's Cry Baby."

His whisper jolted into her ear and the way he placed his hands on her back felt like hot spiders crawling up and down her spine. Esmae shivered uncontrollably and stepped away, not looking at him.

"Hey, I'm teasing," he smiled and lifted his hands up as not to offend her. "You know you're overreacting. I didn't mean to startle you."

Esmae's rapid heartbeat echoed her ache and conflict.

She was sure greeting her like this was and had been an endearment to him. During their decades of marriage, there were times she had shed tears. But since Valentine's Day, when she couldn't stop crying, and the next day when he told her to move out and started divorce proceedings, "Cry Baby" epitomized his obvious and blatant disregard of Esmae's tears and grief. Her world, while not perfect, was something they had together, a family. Now, their lives were forever changed and she cried at the loss of what had been and what could have been, what she imagined future holidays with her kids and grandkids would have been like all together, as a family.

Sparky hadn't felt the same, about anything. When he used this endearment during their relationship, he would pinch her, hard, leaving bruises all over her arms, stomach, legs, and butt. He called them his "love pats" and said marking her showed how much he cared about her.

Before having kids, there were no "love pats" and he hadn't hurt her. After having three children and gaining weight, the frequency of the love pinches increased. Esmae stayed, because they didn't happen often and they were the only way he hurt her physically. He didn't punch or beat her.

Our marriage hasn't been that bad, Esmae reminded herself. *Not compared to others*. Besides, she had no means of supporting their children on her own.

Not being pinched was a benefit of months of living on her own. And the bruises were all healed.

For the sake of the lawyers and fact he may be recording this interaction, like last time, Esmae said nothing confrontational. Then, with a deep sigh of resignation, Esmae turned, her lips drawn into a fake smile which did not reach the look of her sad, disillusioned eyes.

"Hello, Sparky." Esmae's bright tone was another fake mask. The last recording, where he goaded her into an argument, had been damning evidence.

He took a step toward her. She took a breath and held her ground, not backing away. At five feet and nine inches, his slender physique created an illusion of being taller. He leaned down four inches, blew in her face, smirked as it made Esmae close her eyes, then turned and pretended to be interested in a book resting on the cart she was putting away.

From the side, Esmae quickly noted his dark brown hair wasn't grey, not even at the temples, not even a few streaks here and there. His younger girlfriend must have dyed his hair and trimmed his bangs, allowing a clear view of the scar above his right eye which caused his eyebrow to droop more with each decade.

Esmae wondered if Sparky had told his girlfriend of how the scar happened, of how it was proof of his love for her. How, during their senior year, Sparky came to her house one night with blood gushing down his face, both eyes black and blue, a broken nose, and his shirt ruined, drenched with blood. He told her he had defended her honor. When she pressed for details, he insisted he wouldn't tell because it would upset her. She needed to trust him and his love for her. In that moment he was her knight in shining armor, and she believed he always would be. Because she felt loved and protected, she trusted him without any more questions.

Even then, Sparky's stubbornness meant no amount of coaxing would make him go get stitches, which made the skin overlap and the scar heal crooked. During the next decades, the scar was only brought up when Sparky wanted to remind her of how he had fought for her, that's how much he loved her.

"Aw, sweetie," Sparky said, shaking his head in mock disappointment. "No Papi? No Papa Smurf?"

Some men like to be called "Daddy", but not him. From the beginning of their marriage, he wanted his wife and kids to call him "Papa Smurf". Esmae learned last year why being called "Papa Smurf" was important to Sparky. For decades, his Belgium grandparents sent him Smurf comic books and, since no one in the U.S. knew about the Smurfs and the kind, wise, old Papa Smurf until 1981, Sparky relished feeling secretly superior and more knowledgeable than anyone else.

He didn't like being called Sparky. But Esmae would never call him "Papi" or "Papa Smurf" again.

Esmae closed her eyes and reminded herself about being Minnesota nice. They had three beautiful children. He hadn't always broken her heart...had he? And, they were still married.

"Albert is here," he whispered to her as Esmae's eyes

were closed.

She knew what this meant, time to play even nicer. Esmae opened her eyes. Sparky took the last half step toward her, arms outstretched.

"It's nice to see you, too," Sparky laughed with no defensiveness in his demeanor. He projected a casual nonchalant attitude in front of their son, who stood at the end of the aisle behind him.

Sparky wrapped his arms around her. Esmae shook her head impulsively, knowing she didn't have to, but couldn't find the strength to stop him from hugging her. She sighed in resignation, knowing she wouldn't say "no", not in front of their youngest son. They both knew she knew he knew it.

Within another second, Sparky crushed her to him. Esmae wondered if he felt any warmth. She felt a chasm of cold distance and an ache for what had been. Her son looked at them, and Esmae felt the awkwardness of the situation. He knew they no longer lived together and this long-ish, intimate embrace was a bit weird.

Esmae smiled at him over Sparky's shoulder and waved with both hands, finessing a way not to hug Sparky back.

Ah, my son. Esmae gushed at the sight of him. *Taller than his dad, dark hair, leather jacket, and* The Lord of the Rings *under his arm. Like James Dean, but studious without the cigarettes.* She thought.

"He's watching," Sparky whispered in her ear. "Hug me." Instead, she patted his back like burping a baby. He pulled back and pinched the back of her arm, twisting hard. The glare in his eyes dared her to say something, anything.

"Oh, what's this?" He moved to pinch Esmae's side and shook. "This is all that red meat, isn't it? I warned you. You're so...," Sparky looked her up and down, "rounded." He spoke in hushed tones so their son couldn't hear. "You'd be so pretty if you just lost weight...and did something about those wrinkles."

"I haven't changed in the last two days." As thin as Sparky was, Esmae was the opposite. Kids, eating her emotions, stress, and not getting enough exercise had made her an overly plump, middle aged mom.

"Hmmmm, my mis..." Sparky stopped. "Wait. Are you trying to be sarcastic?" With a slight dismissive smile, he turned and took a couple steps to the counter and picked up a package of Esmae's candied nuts. "I could never tell. You're still really bad at that. Despite the fact you work here now. Hmm, this is a step up then, huh?" He untied the string at the top, letting it drop to the floor. Then he proceeded to put a small handful of nuts in his mouth and chew. His eyes never left Esmae, carefully observing her movements. A slight smile started as he watched her squirm and wring her hands. With bravado, he continued talking with nuts in his mouth. "See what I did there? That was real sarcasm." Sparky pressed his lips into a thin, humorless smile and winked at Esmae. Without a sound the message was sent, his ten thousand wins to maybe her two. He would always win.

Sparky swallowed and put more nuts in his mouth, chewing loudly. "Hmmm, these aren't your best," he said, putting another handful in his mouth.

Esmae wasn't sure if she had been trying to be sarcastic. Not changing physically in two days was fact. "Do you want something or are you here to harass me?" Esmae tried to grab the package from him, and he laughed at her attempt as he held it away from her. "You could pay me for those."

"I'm here to pick up our son."

"He's only been here a few minutes," Esmae panicked a bit. "I get to spend some time with him after school, you know this. You don't get him right away."

Without answering Sparky started to walk down the aisle toward their son, mumbling under his breath so Esmae was forced to follow him. "I'm here to find a book for my girlfriend. I mean a girl who's a friend." Sparky smiled at his son. "I'm not sure this, er, um…," he pretended to fumble for the right term. "Hmmm…*quaint* store could hold anything of interest."

Having been with him for one too many years, Esmae understood when he said "quaint" he meant "inconsequential" and "not sophisticated enough" for him or his girlfriend. Rubbing her presence in, even though they were still married.

"Then…" Esmae started, but he turned the corner at the end of the aisle. Through sparse holes in the shelves, she saw him quickly walk and turn in two shelves over.

Walking swiftly back to the other end of the row, Esmae turned cut him off two rows down. "Then leave." She confronted him. "But Albert stays here until we're done." The angry pounding of her heart belied the courage it took to stand up to him.

In a session a few days ago, the therapist told Esmae she allowed herself to be a victim and Sparky, and others, didn't control how she acted or reacted. Her words didn't ring true in these situations.

Sparky glared at Esmae and dug his fingers painfully into her arm, not letting go when she grimaced. "Why do you make me do things like this to you?" he growled.

The cacophony of the door's opening squeak and the bell's jangle were met with high-pitched lyrics, "Oh, Papi Smurfikins."

Sparky let go of Esmae's arm, but stood over her, glaring down into her face, daring her to say something…anything.

"I couldn't wait any longer. It was getting lonely and cold in the car without you," her voice trailed off. "Oh, hi, Albert. Do you know…"

Sparky's face softened. Bending down he whispered in Esmae's ear, "You know I can't live without you." And kissed her cheek, then a quick peck on the lips, coating them with the sweet taste of pumpkin spice nuts. "I love you. Always. Remember that."

He turned as his girlfriend came down the aisle they were on. Long legs in a short skirt and tight tank top emphasized her slender body with curves in the right places. She completed the look with an oversized, black Elizabeth Taylor hat, dark sunglasses, and red lipstick which would have been perfect as a picture on the cover of *Seventeen* or *Vogue*, but not so much in small town Detroit Lakes.

Esmae stood stunned and motionless during Sparky and his girlfriend's loud "mwah", and the girlfriend's subsequent giggle. They had kissed, in Myrtle's store, in front of her. Luckily, Albert was perusing the books and oddities somewhere else in the store.

"But, Sweetikins," his voice flowed like smooth maple syrup, unlike the rough, threatening bark of moments before with Esmae. "I haven't found you a gift yet."

"You bought me that glass sea vase at the last store," she cooed and Esmae heard her kiss him on the cheek.

"It's beautiful. Thank you."

"I buy you three presents every week," he spoke louder. Esmae knew it was so she could hear. "Tomorrow is Saturday, so there's one more present to get you. Though, there might not be anything in here," he said as he led her away. "From the outside, this looked like an eclectic bookstore, but it's plain. Why don't you wait outside? I have a few things to finish up."

"But…"

He put his finger to her lips. "No buts, my sweet Desiree. Be a good girl and do what Papi says. We'll find you a present elsewhere."

Albert appeared at the end of the aisle and Sparky kissed her forehead instead of her lips.

"Off you go," he turned her around and smacked her bottom.

Albert smiled at Desiree as she walked by, then started to follow her out.

"Albert, where are you going?" Sparky said.

Albert stopped and looked back, first at his mom then his dad, then at his mom again. "I…," Albert hesitated, "I was just walking her to the car." He stood tall and silent.

"Aren't you supposed to spend some time with your mom?"

"Yeah." Albert wasn't sure how to answer this so his dad wouldn't get pissed off.

"Then, after a few minutes come back and I'll see you tonight…," Sparky looked back at Esmae then to their son. "Or tomorrow for soccer."

Albert smiled. "Ok. Thanks, Dad!" He walked outside to talk with his dad's girlfriend.

The overly stacked books created a dark, looming hall as Sparky walked toward Esmae. She backed up and went behind the books she had been putting away. Across the cart from each, the fear, hurt, and sadness in her eyes made him hesitate.

"Esmae, look, I'm sorry," a flicker of something passed through his eyes and his eyebrows burrowed. "We had some good times. I was good to you…" and his words trailed off as he bent his head slightly to the right in contemplation.

Esmae wanted to say, "No, you were Shitty Smurf," but her throat constricted into silence. She knew saying this or anything would anger him and he would relish arguing the point, especially giving more ammunition to his side of the story for the lawyers and for all of their friends and co-workers. People who would never be her friends again because they chose his version. There was no way for Esmae to defend herself. She believed he would change too many times before. Decades of the church telling her, be obedient, the man is the king of the home, love conquers all. She had tried, and there were good times. She had loved him with all of her being, and, in some ways, still loved him and wanted the future she had been working toward for all their decades together.

And Sparky could be charming, even to her.

To deal with his charm, Esmae knew she couldn't argue with him and win. Silence was her only weapon.

"Hello there, boy," Myrtle floated in from a secret passage from behind the counter.

"Lady Myrtle," Sparky said with cold, distant respect. "You know me. And you know how much I hate being called boy."

Myrtle ignored him.

"As much as we'd like to help you today, the shop is closing early. Thanks for coming in." She glided around the cart. Even though Sparky stood a good foot taller than her, this did not dissuade Myrtle. Not looking at him, she turned him with a hand on his arm and another lightly behind his back. Her small statue didn't seem strong, but the touch of her hand and the force of her presence dazzled and surrounded him with complacency. Sparky couldn't resist being guided toward the door.

Esmae followed them.

The bell twinkled as he left, filling the dark aura he brought with cleansing, dusty, white sparkles. The light from the open door scattered any darkness and flooded Esmae with relief.

"We need to do a cleansing," Myrtle said as she started to shut and lock the door.

"My son…"

Myrtle held the doorknob and pulled Esmae to her. "One day, you're going to have to stand up for yourself." The intensity and meaning with which she spoke hit Esmae to her core. Absolutely, without a doubt, Myrtle was right. But Esmae didn't and couldn't hear it.

The "Yes," came out as a squeak as Esmae continued finding her voice again.

Myrtle stepped beside Esmae as Albert opened the door and the bell rang.

"Aw," Myrtle patted his arm. "Nice to see you, Al…Bert." She spoke as if Albert were two separate first names.

"I am grateful to you."

"I know, dear."

They smiled knowingly at each other.

"Did you make tea?" Esmae smiled bigger at this sweet, intuitive lady.

"Oh, why yes," Myrtle looked surprised at the remembrance. "Be ready in a minute." She hurried off to the kitchen. "Your mug is the one painted with the soccer ball. Right, Al…Bert?"

"Yes, ma'am," was Albert surprised response. He hadn't been in the bookstore in over a year or spent time alone with his mom in a few weeks.

"And some scones with that peach jam you brought?"

Esmae hugged her son to her. "We would love to." Albert groaned and Esmae reached up and attempted to rustle his hair. "You will love this. So many great stories."

Stacks of books and other oddities sparkled faintly, almost as a greeting, as Myrtle then Albert and his mom walked by, making the floating specks seem like fairy dust.

Chapter 3

"Was the game cancelled?" Myrtle asked as she handed Esmae a clean rag.

Esmae reached for it, paused, and inhaled deeply. Squishing her nostrils together, she tried to hold in the sneeze. Myrtle softly flicked the rag at her.

"Let it out," she said. "You don't want your brains to explode."

With that, Esmae turned away from Myrtle and sneezed with such a forceful sneeze it moved a cloud of dust into the air. A gust of wind from the open door allowed the swirl of dust to be sucked outside into the heavy rain and disappear.

"Uff da," Esmae said, wiping her nose with a nearby tissue. "Sorry."

"No, no, sweetie. You go ahead, blow that dust away," Myrtle chuckled as she wiped her finger across a book and shrugged her shoulders. "Tsk. Tsk. Can't believe these books gather dust so quickly."

Esmae agreed, taking the clean rag from Myrtle and

continuing to wipe the dust off the new donations. "Having these two estates donate the last few weeks adds to the collection. Have you sorted most of the boxes?"

Myrtle shook her head no. "So glad you could come in early." She paused, then placed a hand on Esmae's shoulder. "And sorry about it, too."

Esmae felt the warmth of Myrtle's touch, then a comforting pat. "It's okay," Esmae attempted a smile. "Al and I had a wonderful night. His dad..."

"I know, dear, I know," Myrtle squeezed and patted Esmae's shoulder. "Tea?"

Esmae laughed. Myrtle's remedy for anything was strong black tea and biscuits or scones with Esmae's homemade raspberry or peach brandy jam.

"Yes, please."

"Be done in a jiffy," Myrtle said, already halfway down the aisle. "We need fresh scones with piping hot tea on a day like today."

Which meant Esmae had about an hour to dust and clean the rest of the donations, so they could fully relax by the fire.

A clap of thunder rattled the windows and a flash of lightening lit up the shop for an instant.

"Uff, that was close," Esmae yelled back to the kitchen, hoping she wouldn't have to yell louder.

Myrtle's "No worries, dear" seemed to echo through

the canyon of books. "This store has survived worse."

Indeed, it had. The flood of '76 and the cluster of sixteen tornadoes throughout Minnesota in '79, both devastated homes and businesses in the area. The sandbags and the bookstore being elevated on a hill had kept its basement from flooding. Enough to save the place. Luckily, the three tornadoes from the South, turned at the lake, and faded before reaching the shoppe. The Red Cross set up next to Myrtle's bookstore, and she made tea, scones, and sandwiches for the crew, volunteers, firefighters, and families stunned by the loss.

Having grown up in Detroit Lakes, Esmae knew Myrtle and perused the bookstore a few times as a teen. But it wasn't until after the tornadoes that Esmae connected with Myrtle personally and started visiting the shoppe and, well, Myrtle, more often. When she separated and Sparky told her to move out, Myrtle rented her the small seven-hundred-foot cottage, the first home Earl and Myrtle owned, and hired Esmae on a part-time basis, but the hours tended to be full-time.

Esmae didn't mind. Life was different with her 29-year-old daughter in a different state and her 25-year-old son living on his own in Fargo. Those changes made the house quieter. Each of her children was unplanned, but deeply wanted. None more of a surprise than Albert who, at sixteen, was usually busy with his friends and sports.

Living on her own without Sparky and Albert made life less stressful, but much lonelier. There were some things about her previous life she truly missed and, if she was honest, would do anything to have back, to fill that hole in her heart at not having her family together.

Thunder shook the bookstore again. Another flash of lightening blinded Esmae for a second as it struck a powerline less than a block away. Holding on to the bookshelf, she steadied herself until her eyes adjusted to the darkness.

"Myrtle," Esmae said loudly. A single light bobbed like a ball from the back toward her.

"Right here."

The light rounded the corner, beamed in her eyes for a second, blinding her again, before Myrtle lowered the flashlight to shine on the worn oak floors. "Oops, sorry."

Esmae couldn't see Myrtle's face, but heard her soft voice next to her.

"I think the fuses may be fried."

"Give me a sec, Myrtle," said Esmae. "I'll take care of it." Myrtle's hand on Esmae's arm created a warmth which surged through her.

Within a few seconds, Esmae's eyes adjusted and she saw the gentle smile of Myrtle and the lines of her face dimly lit by the downward, dispersed glow of the flashlight.

Myrtle handed her an extra flashlight.

"Has to be…. Well," Myrtle said, almost answering Esmae's thoughts, "you know where the circuit breaker is."

Esmae shuddered. Yep, in the dark, eerie basement with all the weirder oddities and curiosities that would — and had — scared most customers away. That's why they were in the basement. She took the flashlight and with a weak bravado said, "Back in a flash. Hehe."

"Tally ho," Myrtle cheerily responded.

Esmae patted Myrtle's arm as she walked by. As grown women, there was no reason to fear the spidery, dusty, creepy basement.

A shiver shuddered again down her spine. Grimacing, Esmae stepped onto the first step descending into the black hole, the flashlight barely piercing the darkness beyond a step or two.

Chapter 4

Esmae flipped the circuit switch again. "Myrtle," she yelled loud enough to make her throat ache from the strain. "Anything?"

A hollow "no" echoed down to her. Then a faint mumble and all Esmae could understand was "...go ...Kevin..." and more words.

"What?"

The word, "Back...," echoed down and faint, indistinguishable mumbling, then nothing.

The silence intensified the darkness surrounding Esmae. Turning, she flashed the flashlight around. On the wall a few feet away, she noticed a small window toward the ceiling which was supposed to let light in. The storm clouds and the late evening made that impossible.

Slowly she scanned the basement with the narrow, weak range of the flashlight, trying to find the path to the stairs. Getting there had gone quicker then she imagined it would. She kept to the left, but made a few turns when the path was blocked. Meandering through this haphazard mesh of tables and bookshelves stacked with odds and ends disoriented her on the way to the circuit box. With tentative steps, she stepped in the direction she thought the stairs should be.

Straight this way and then a couple turns? She tried to remember as she shined the light high, then low, seeing if any of the stacks and shelves looked familiar. She took two steps and walked straight into a table with a box filled with naked porcelain baby dolls and, lying on top, some detached heads with half-closed eyes, Xs on one or both eyes, or no eyes at all.

Why did all old houses have a box of these creepy porcelain dolls? Where did they all come from? The thought made her scurry in another direction, turn into a row with towering shelves dusty with age, cobwebs, and remembrance. The boxes placed here showed faded labels. Curiosity made Esmae try to read a few, barely making out who the box belonged to. Estate _f Patrick O'Ma_le_, B_oks donated by H_ly R__ary C___ch, and many others of estate of something and someone too faded to make out,

Halfway through the basement the bookshelf row was blocked by tables stacked with more boxes, toys, stuffed animals, and clothes. Esmae turned into more bookshelves which contained a row of dirty mason jars with something inside. She wiped the outside and saw a baby pig and a frog and—what the heck—a chicken's head and foot. Alongside this jar was a rabbit's foot and a harmonica covered with dust and cobwebs. A black widow spider crawled out from one of the note holes in the harmonica toward Esmae.

"Jesus, Mary, and Joseph!" She forcibly stepped back into another bookshelf jolting the contents. A box toppled from the top, hitting her shoulder and knocking the flashlight out of her hand to the ground. It clattered and rolled, breaking the light within as it fell apart.

In an instant, the darkness embraced her completely. Esmae lifted her hand and couldn't see in front of her.

Her heart thumped hard and fast in her ears. Tears rolled down her cheeks. Esmae could feel their hotness create lines in the dirt and dust on her face. Her hands shook. This had happened before. Esmae wasn't sure when or where, but this darkness and dust produced a déjà vu moment that terrified her.

She felt the bookshelf pressed against her back. Reaching behind, she used the bookshelf as a guide as she slid to the floor. Taking deeps breaths, Esmae tried to calm the pounding and not think about the spider working its way toward her. *How could something like that survive in a place like this? Were there other bugs?* Esmae shuddered. Closing her eyes, she filled the void with her whisper and another memory activated from decades before.

"Red Rose, proud Rose, sad Rose of all my days.

Come …while I sing the ancient ways," she hesitated. She couldn't remember all of the words. Trying to visual what she could remember distracted her.

"…A…battling with the bitter tide;
The Druid, grey, wood-nurtured, quiet-eyed,
Who cast round…dreams…ruin untold.
My… own sadness, whereof stars, grown old
…dancing silver-sandalled on the sea.
…Come near…no more blinded by man's fate.
I find under the boughs of love and hate,
In all poor foolish things that live a day,
Eternal beauty wandering on her way."

Taking her sleeve, she smeared the tears and dirt at her jowl line. Slowly repeating her favorite images, picturing each one, her Irish narrator joined in. *Red Rose, proud Rose, sad Rose…I sing the ancient ways…Druid, grey, wood-nurtured and quiet-eyed… stars grown old… dancing silver-sandalled on the sea… not blinded by man's fate… I find… boughs of love and hate… poor foolish things…eternal beauty…wandering on her way.*

The Irish voice continued to join Esmae as she kept repeating these images until her heart slowed allowing her to hear the heavy rain and thunder outside. These comforted and calmed her further. Who knew a Yeats' poem learned in senior English would come back to her thirty years later at a moment like this.

Esmae took a deep breath, held it as she calmed herself further, then exhaled. Taking another deep breath, the Irish voice echoed the poem's imagery.

As Esmae let it resonate throughout her being, a glimmer pierced her thoughts and the darkness surrounding her. The constant light contrasted with the faint flash from lightning. Opening her eyes, she looked to her right and saw the soft glow coming from the box that had dropped and hit her hand. The box was on its side and the glow faintly illuminated the outline and shadows of items scattered on the floor. Esmae focused intensely on the glow in an attempt to ignore the freaky, creepy shapes their shadows made on the floor and shelves. With only one hand, she reached sideways toward the box. The weight and size made it impossible to turn the box upright. Tears welled, blurring everything, distorting the shadows even more. Esmae knew she couldn't give into her fear.

The floor dug into her knees as Esmae knelt beside the box, took an aggressive stance, and, using both hands, grasped the side of the box and turned it upright.

Esmae gasped as the items in the box toppled back on top of the light and extinguished it. Digging in a box, not knowing what was in it, what living or dead insect or creature she might touch, gave Esmae the heebie-jeebies.

Shaking her head, swallowing, and swallowing some

more, she reached down and touched something furry. Esmae quickly pulled her hand out. Listening for a moment, she determined nothing moved and put her hand back, touching and moving the furry item aside.

The Irish voice began reciting the lines and Esmae whispered them with him as soothing background. *Red Rose, proud Rose, sad Rose…I sing the ancient ways…*

Paper crumbled as she felt a small, hard square wrapped inside. Esmae felt a variety of wrappings as she gingerly touched the objects and placed the items and what they were wrapped in on the floor. As she blindly explored deeper, a few sharp objects poked her. Deep into the box, she touched luxurious, soft velvet. She rubbed it between her fingers, pulling up on its closure to move it aside. The top opened for a second and allowed a beacon of light to emerge, stunning Esmae. For a minute, she closed her eyes to sooth the bright circles, never letting go of the velvet cloth, anxiously not wanting to lose it and dig for it again among the disturbing, unknown items.

With both hands, Esmae pulled the cloth with its weighty contents from the box, then sat back against the bookshelf, and placed it on her lap. The top of the velvet material folded over and protected the object inside. There was a drawstring which had loosened in the fall, but as Esmae tried to pull it open, the drawstring wouldn't budge. Only a small opening allowed the glow to create a pillar of light almost reaching the basement's ceiling.

This was a stronger light than the flashlight, but the small hole and large bag made it impossible to use. Esmae held the top of the velvet bag stiff so the light illuminated the area she was in and awkwardly looked in the box for something to cut the drawstring with. A metal, knife-looking letter opener reflected a glint.

With one hand, Esmae held the top of the velvet bag. With the other hand, Esmae felt for the letter opener, the tip of the letter opener pricking her ring finger.

Sharp thing for being so old, Esmae thought as she grasped the handle. She let go of the bag and plunged the basement into darkness again as the material covered the light inside. After feeling for and finding the knot in the drawstring, Esmae took the letter opener and sawed the piece of string close by the knot. The velvet bag fell open, exposing the full force of the glowing treasure.

Relief flooded Esmae like the light flooding the basement. The Irish voice's final words joined in driving the rest of the thick, black presence away.

When the wind has laughed and murmured and sung,
The lonely of heart is withered away.

Chapter 5

"Are you okay, dear?" Myrtle hurried to Esmae, who sat in an oversized chair in front of a roaring fireplace drinking piping hot tea. Dust streaked Esmae's face and covered her hair and clothes with an obvious, uncomfortable layer.

"Thank god for a gas stove," Esmae raised her cup in a tiny salute to Myrtle. When she brought it to her lips, it shook, betraying any mock confidence.

"Hey, Izzy," Kevin said, standing tall and muscular in his black firehouse uniform.

"Hey, Kev," Esmae lifted her head slightly in acknowledgment then continued to stare into the fire and sip her tea.

Both Kevin and Myrtle stood drenched and dripping from the rain. Kevin guided Myrtle to the adjacent chair.

Myrtle sneezed.

"Do you…" Esmae and Kevin said at the same time and glanced at each other.

"Yes, please," Myrtle said. Esmae started to get up,

but Kevin was already walking away.

"I know where everything is," he said. "Is the pot still hot, Izzy?"

Esmae sat back down. Twice in one day. No one used that nickname any more, not for years, decades even. They weren't in high school anymore. Though, he would always be her first boyfriend.

"Yes," she said. Using his nickname "Pipe" which he earned being a volunteer fireman as a teen, would make Esmae uncomfortable.

The fire warmed Esmae and Myrtle both as they sat silently. Myrtle looked expectantly at Esmae but didn't ask.

"Here's your tea, Lady Myrtle. Two sugars, a splash of milk," Kevin sat the cup and its saucer next to her on the table between the two ladies.

Myrtle opened her mouth and Kevin produced another sugar cube and dropped it into her tea. "Two sugars had a baby," he winked at her. "I'll go check that circuit board."

Myrtle patted his arm in thanks. Kevin walked past Esmae and spied a blanket on the couch, grabbed it, and went back to tuck it around Myrtle's shoulders.

"Be careful," Esmae said. "A box accidentally spilled, and its contents are all over."

"Good to know," Kevin said, flipped on his hat's light,

placed it on his head, then grabbed a flashlight from his pants pocket. Both illuminated the area more than the fire.

"It's really creepy down there," Esmae's hands still shook some as she sipped her tea.

Without another word, Kevin left them to deal with the circuit breaker and break the gloomy darkness of the basement.

Hot tea languidly soothed Esmae's nerves and warmed Myrtle, who was wet and chilled to the bone.

A few more sips and Esmae began to share with Myrtle. The darkness, the jars, the spider, the box, and the glowing light inside a velvet bag that helped her find her way out of the basement.

"You're safe now, dear," Myrtle said as she stared at the fire, mirroring Esmae and sipping her tea in contemplation.

Esmae pulled out the dark purple bag tucked alongside her and placed it on the table between them. The velvet belied a newness which didn't fit sitting in a box for ages. The drawstring tightened at the top into a peak and what was inside bulged the bottom.

"May I?" asked Myrtle.

Esmae shrugged her shoulders. Everything in the shop Myrtle owned, including what the bag contained. Myrtle pulled a string to loosen the bow and the drawstring fell away. The velvet cloth draped around an ink bottle topped with a shiny metal ornament lid. Lifting it up, Myrtle felt the weight and smooth, clear glass which revealed dark ink inside. Nothing glowed.

"This looks like one of those ink well bottles used with an old fashion dipping pen," Myrtle observed. She felt the etchings on the lid and pen holders. "This design seems familiar. It's a Celtic or Irish, more of an X than a cross, especially with those heart symbols. That's a four-leaf clover with pronounced internal lines and a little twirl inside each leaf." Myrtle mused quietly, almost to herself. "And the two pen holders. I haven't seen that in a long time…" Myrtle trailed off in contemplation.

"That ink glowed downstairs," Esmae said. "When I got back upstairs and lit the fire, it stopped glowing."

Myrtle turned the ink bottle around, upside down, and shook it. Not even shaking made it glow. She handed it to Esmae, who held out her hand. As soon as Myrtle placed the bottle on Esmae's palm, the ink began to glow. They both gasped. Myrtle lifted the ink bottle and it glowed only faintly. She placed it back on the table between them. The closer the ink well was to Esmae, the more it lit the space between them like a small lighthouse beacon shining out from all four sides of the bottle.

"Jimmy Christmases," Myrtle said, this was the closest to swearing Esmae had heard from her.

Esmae brought the ink bottle to her. Turning it in

every direction as Myrtle had, the ink swayed and tumbled but continued to glow. She shook it. The glow neither diminished nor increased.

"Wait," Myrtle said. Forgetting the wet and chill, she let the blanket drop to the floor as she hurried to one of the display cases. Taking a plain, glass dip pen and a small notebook, she placed them on the table.

Esmae placed the ink bottle on the table next to them. When she let go, the ink bottle's glow faded to a lightening bug. She grasped the lid, and the glow increased. The lid stuck as Esmae tried twisting with her right hand, then her left, then her right again. The lid wouldn't budge.

They stared at the faintly glowing ink bottle as it sat on the table between them. They didn't hear Kevin squat down between them and stare at the bottle.

"What are we waiting for?" he finally whispered. "I don't think it is going to move. Pretty cool, though, glow-in-the-dark ink."

Startled, Myrtle put her hand to her heart. "Oh, Kevin, bless my soul. Dearest, don't do that."

"Could you…would you," Esmae asked, "open it?" She didn't want to hand him the bottle and make the glow stronger. This seemed like something she needed to keep as a secret, for now.

Kevin grasped the bottle and twisted the lid with ease.

He placed it back on the table and lifted the lid revealing black ink around the rim and an intoxicating aroma of lavender and rosemary emerged, mingling with the scent of chamomile tea. Kevin placed the lid on the table. They inhaled deeply, the smell relaxing them.

For a few minutes, Esmae resisted the urge to touch the bottle and try the ink pen while Myrtle and Kevin talked about the circuit board and how it was fried from the lightning and some of the fuses were melted. The whole thing needed to be replaced. He could do it, but it would have to wait until Monday when he and his friend, Pete, were off duty.

"Do you have a place to stay?" Kevin asked.

"She can stay with me," Esmae said.

"I'll be perfectly fine here," Myrtle protested.

"No, you won't," Kevin said. "The weather is going to continue to get colder and there won't be any lights or heat on."

"Fine, fine," Myrtle waved her hand. "Would you mind helping me? I'll need your light to gather a few of my things." Myrtle patted Esmae's arm, then led Kevin to the kitchen and the stairs leading to the second story and her living quarters.

Esmae reached for the glass pen, pulled the ink well towards her making the ink glow stronger, and dipped the pen in. The ink didn't glow when she held the pen.

The ink didn't stay on the pen when she pulled it out, and when she tried to write her name on the notepad, there was nothing. Esmae tried again. Nothing. She touched the bottle, the ink glowed. She touched the lid. The ink didn't glow until she placed the lid back on the bottle.

As she heard voices and footsteps approach, Esmae screwed the lid back on the ink well.

"Ready?" Myrtle asked as they approached Esmae.

"Yeah."

"Should we bring this with?" Myrtle indicated the ink bottle, pen, and notepad.

"No," Esmae stood, gathered a shawl around her, and looked at Myrtle. "The ink doesn't work." Her brow furrowed in puzzlement.

Myrtle placed the ink bottle back in the velvet bag and tied the string into a bow. Then she handed the items to Esmae. "Let's bring them with, just because."

After locking up, Kevin gave them a ride to the cottage along North Shore Drive without asking directions.

Interesting he knows where I live without asking me for directions. Esmae wondered what else he knew about her life without her saying anything.

During the next day and two nights, Myrtle shared memories of living in the cottage when she was first married to Earl.

And they pondered why the ink only glowed when Esmae was close to or touched the bottle.

Chapter 6

"You have great tapu, my dear," Myrtle said as they gathered the dirty dishes from the table after Sunday dinner and put them in the sink to wash them.

"Tapu?"

"A Māori term for spiritual power," Myrtle explained, running the water while Esmae took out the dish drying rack and a towel to dry. "Other cultures have other names, such as manitou among the Algonquian, mana uhane in Hawaiian, and slí an chroí used by the Irish Celtic Shamans."

Esmae's frown deepened the lines between her eyes and her face squished in disbelieving curiosity. Never had she considered having any sort of spiritual power. That didn't happen to people like her.

Myrtle rinsed a glass and handed it to Esmae to dry.

"For our honeymoon, Earl and I went to New Zealand," Myrtle explained and told of how they travelled there because of an article she had read in National Geographic. An adventure solidifying her love of all things curious, unique, and out of the ordinary. "I found their connection to the spiritual world powerful and different than anything we experienced before."

"But, that's them," Esmae said, taking a plate from the drying rack, wiping it, and stacking it on the counter to be put away later.

"Tapu is just a term," Myrtle said as she put the last of the dishes in the sink to wash. "Anyone can have tapu. You don't have to be Māori."

"I'm a Christian."

"Are you? Or are you more spiritual?" Myrtle said matter-of-factly while handing Esmae a pan to dry.

Esmae had to admit Myrtle was right. She used the label Christian, but much of what she practiced had nothing to do with a religion but with what she felt.

"Then you believe in spirituality and intuition?"

"Yes," Esmae hesitated in answering.

"Don't you think spirituality and intuition cross cultural borders and we aren't bound by religious laws?"

Wrapping her head around this made her headache, but in principle Esmae agreed. Religion and spirituality were different in practice and essence.

"Then your connection with the ink, there is something more to it. Something that transcends religious limits and restraints," Myrtle finished rinsing the soap off the last few dishes and her hands. Leaving them on the drying rack, she turned to Esmae and placed both hands firmly on her shoulders. A warmth coursed through Esmae's body from her neck to her toes, making her relax and want to melt into a puddle.

"How?" Esmae marvelled. "I don't have power like that."

"Not dominating, controlling power," Myrtle took the towel and dish from Esmae's hand before she dropped them. "But a spiritual connection, which is inherent throughout world. Generally, people aren't aware of their connection. This spirituality connects more strongly in some. This must be what is happening with you."

They walked a few steps into the living room and sat on the couch facing the fire. Myrtle on one side, Esmae on the other. The rain pelted the roof and a few drops sizzled when it fell through the chimney onto the crackling fire.

Barely above a whisper, Myrtle began to speak. "But there are spirits that want to steal it, to harness it as their own. When you have relations with these malevolent spirits, it can take years for your own spirit and its intuitive connection to recover."

Esmae couldn't look at Myrtle. She was embarrassed by who she fell in love with, but, on some level, she still wanted that life with him. For decades she had accepted the positives as well as the negatives of what it meant to be resigned to this life with Sparky. Yes, she was embarrassed that part of her still wanted the life she had. There was stability in it.

Her heart ached for what could have been, if only.... She blamed Sparky, and her parents. But mostly, she blamed herself. Part of her still loved Sparky.

Myrtle slid over and took both of Esmae's hands in hers. When Esmae got upset, her body became cold. She didn't realize how cold she was until the warmth of Myrtle's hands coursed through her again.

"There are some things you can blame on them, and others you can't. What you can do is tear apart those hurts and deal with them, then heal."

"Don't give me platitudes. Please," Esmae shook her head, squeezed Myrtle's hands, and released them. A sob caught in her throat as she continued. "I don't want to hear some awful optimistic quotes about how 'what doesn't kill us makes us stronger' or that 'don't worry, be happy, things will get better.' I'm just so tired of those. I think I've been strong enough for too long, by myself. I don't want it to take so much effort. At this time, I just want these trials to kill me and get it over with," Esmae cried uncontrollable sobs. Where had this tirade come from? The depth of her hurts, the rejections, abandonment, the abuse, seemed to culminate into a sharp point.

"I'm sorry," Esmae said between sobs. She looked at

Myrtle's gentle, wrinkled face. "I didn't mean it. Forgive me."

"It's okay," Myrtle patted Esmae's leg. "All part of finding your voice, recognizing what you've gone through, and healing...connecting with your spirit and soul-self again."

They sat listening to the rain, each lost in their own thoughts and contemplations.

"Okay," Myrtle got up. "Let's look at this ink bottle again. Where did you put it?"

After finding it in Esmae's coat pocket, Myrtle placed the ink well in Esmae's hand and it glowed on cue.

"Fascinating," Myrtle said, then took it and placed it in her own. No glow commenced. Placing it back on Esmae's palm, the ink bottle illuminated like fireflies captured in a bottle. "There is a connection between you. Destiny has spiritual influence and intuition. You were destined for each other."

Despite her skepticism, Esmae decided not to contradict Myrtle. If destiny or fate was part of a person's life, then her parents were destined to die? Sparky was meant to hurt and cheat on her? They were meant to be together, and she was meant to go through these years of losing her sense of purpose and not knowing herself? Or not being supported and put down by someone she had considered to be the love of her life? Her true and once-in-a-lifetime love? That was no more. Or should she not give up on him?

"Was there a pen with it?" Myrtle interrupted Esmae's thoughts. "There should have been a pen with it. Since this pen doesn't work."

"I don't know," a sudden feeling of being overwhelmed spun hard in Esmae's head. The dizziness made her not be able to think straight.

Myrtle embraced her, folding Esmae onto her shoulder. After a few minutes, Esmae felt uncomfortable and tried to pull away, Myrtle wouldn't let her.

"Let it all out," she said. "I love you as you are. As vulnerable as you are in this moment. Just a few more minutes." She smoothed Esmae's hair and rubbed her back. Esmae remembered seeing moms do this to their children. She couldn't remember it ever being done to her. And she cried at all the things she missed.

"To everything there is a season and that prepares us for the future," Myrtle said squeezing Esmae in a final embrace, then releasing her. "As Marilyn Monroe said, things fall apart so better things can come together."

"Ha," Esmae laughed a little at the incredulous thought. "Marilyn Monroe said that?"

"Yes, my dear," Myrtle said. "She wasn't a dumb blonde. She only acted like one." She winked at Esmae.

Esmae looked down at her hands, understanding

what Myrtle was implying but still wasn't sure. "He's the father of my children...," Esme hesitated and continued sheepishly, still looking down at her hands as she rubbed them together for warmth. "I do wonder what destiny has in store for me. Even if that means staying with him." Esmae peeked up at Myrtle, thinking she would reprimand her.

A mischievous, excited smile lit up Myrtle's face. "Oh, sweetheart, I have just what you need."

Chapter 7

Someone has to.

Those words echoed in Esmae's head as she headed back down the narrow stairs into the dismal, dark, fear and spider infested basement. She kept mouthing the words "no, no, no" with each shaky step.

But someone had to, and she wasn't going to have Myrtle do it. In the whole scheme of things, Esmae was the only person who knew where the box was.

Kevin and his friend had replaced the circuit box yesterday, which lit up the rest of the shoppe. But the cave-like basement, along with an overgrown amount of weird items, sucked the light from the three or four lightbulbs to a dimness that made the shadows saturate the floor and corners with darkness. Or maybe she hated weird basements and her fear made the shadows dance in its nooks and crannies. Didn't matter. Esmae had to do this. *Would* do this.

The Irish narrator enhanced the fear Esmae felt, *I dreamed that one had died in a strange place. Near no accustomed hand, And, they had nailed the boards above her face…*

"What!" Esmae exclaimed out loud, not able to contain herself. The Irish voice couldn't be blocked as she covered her ears. The Irish voice continued reciting the poem. Usually, the voice soothed or comforted her. This was decidedly not either of those.

"La la la la la la la la la la la la," Esmae said as loudly as she could to cover the inner Irish voice. Finally, there was a pause and Esmae heard his voice no more. She stopped covering her ears and the monotone singing. Why would her own inner voice do something like that to her? If doubling down on fear was his dry sense of humor, she wasn't sure what to think. Dying in a strange place wasn't something she wanted to think about.

Esmae paused and took a deep breath. Though, the voice did have a point. Would she really die in this basement? Even if it was a dark and spooky place? Probably not.

The pause only lasted for a few seconds when the Irish narrator continued, *I know that I shall meet my fate. Somewhere among the clouds above…*

The narrator continued, but Esmae stopped repeating the words "no, no, no" and, instead, recited his words, "I know that I shall meet my fate" as she descended the last few steps and made her way around the maze of oddities, shelves, and tables. Funny how the Irish narrator could be reciting a poem and she could be focused on the words she was speaking. Two voices in her head at one time. Maybe she was going crazy?

She whispered to herself and, hopefully, to the Irish voice in her head, "I know that I shall meet my fate." The Irish voice began to repeatedly echo her, *I know that I shall meet my fate.* In unison, they said it together as Esmae found the spilled box. The darkness of the floor and towering shelves created an impossible task for Esmae to find anything specific in or around the box, even with her flashlight. With swiftness, she gathered everything that had fallen out or that she had placed on the floor, flashing under the bottom of a few shelves, in case things had rolled beneath them, like the parts of the flashlight she had dropped.

Hoping she wouldn't find any spiders or other creepy crawlies, Esmae still took the time to be thorough in her search. She didn't want to come down here again.

The weight of the box strained Esmae's back and arms. She tried different positions, but couldn't lift it and hold on to the flashlight at the same time. As a last resort, Esmae did the only thing she could think of, she put the end of the flashlight in her mouth, squatted down, and lifted the box with her legs and back. The metal of the flashlight made her mouth water and, as Esmae walked, she found it bounced too much for it to be much use. She dropped the flashlight in the box, where it shined in the corner, illuminating dust, not helping Esmae find her way.

I know that I shall meet my fate, the Irish voice repeated. Esme took a deep breath of relief. She wasn't alone. Whoever he was, this spiritual connection, this kismet, his Irish voice kept her company.

Squinting in the dim light, Esmae couldn't see the ground and it was impossible to navigate any distance beyond a foot or two with all the shelves in the way. Sliding one tentative, hesitant step forward at a time, Esmae took her time managing the basement maze.

I know that I shall meet my fate. They whispered it together as slowly, carefully, Esmae made her way back to the stairs.

Having lost all sense of time, Esmae stood on the landing at the top of the stairs not knowing how long it had taken to get there or how many times they had echoed those lines to each other as she made her way beyond the gloom and fear of the basement. What Esmae did know is she would never forget them or the feeling she was beginning to believe there was something more to them than how they comforted her.

"Hey, there" Kevin said as he came through the

bathroom to the basement door and landing. "I was just coming to help you. Myrtle told me you'd been gone for a bit." He reached out and brushed off some cobwebs from Esmae's head.

"Oops," Kevin raised his eyebrows at her. "Look at me, Izzy. Stay calm."

She couldn't help herself. Esmae glanced over, saw him scoop a large, black spider from her shoulder, and screamed as she backed away from them into the corner. The thud of her body with the weight of the box rattled the shelves and toppled off a few of the bathroom and cleaning supplies.

Swiftly, Kevin took the spider, opened the window to the bathroom, and let it outside. In a second, he was back grabbing the box and Esmae's arm.

"You're okay," he said. "I've got you. Still terrified of spiders, eh?" Kevin eyes twinkled as he tried not to smile.

"And you know why," Esmae's eyes narrowed. If her hands had been free, she would have playfully punched him in the arm.

Indeed, he did know why. Kevin didn't say another word, but took the box from Esmae.

Despite the weight and size of the box, what took Esmae two arms to lift, Kevin did with one. Putting it on his shoulder, he stood aside and motioned for Esmae to lead the way through the bathroom to the shoppe and fireplace where Myrtle sat in one of the large, comfortable wingback chairs upholstered not in flowers, like so many were, but with a book design.

Kevin placed the box on the floor in front of the fireplace and between the two ladies, then sat on the edge of the couch. Esmae sat in the other wingback chair.

"Well, anyone curious?" Kevin broke the silence after a few minutes of staring at the box. He was a doer, not one to sit around staring contemplatively at the box imaging what might be in it. He wanted to find out.

Contemplation was exactly what Myrtle and Esmae were doing. Myrtle pondered where the box came from, for many had donated to her and Earl over the years. Vaguely it felt familiar, for Myrtle's intuition was good about these things. Maybe Earl was cleaning the clutter and didn't tell Myrtle he was storing it in the basement. Maybe looking at the contents would bridge the familiar with a solid remembrance.

Esmae sat wondering what kind of fate this box held for her. What if this, too, would end in disappointment and failure? The familiar was comforting. The unknown scared her. Esmae pressed her lips together, intrigued and reluctant.

"Does that mean you don't want to look inside?" Kevin asked, watching Esmae. "You brought it up for...decoration? Halloween is in another six weeks or so," Kevin chuckled. The dusty box fit into the Halloween feel and the decades of famous Haunted Houses held in Myrtle's shoppe. Of all the Haunted Houses, people talked about her 'Little Shoppe of Horrors' for months.

One year the items Myrtle displayed gave kids nightmares and disturbed the parents to such a degree they called on the Mayor Norm to see if they were real or not. Myrtle assured him they weren't, but Kevin and every other child wasn't so sure. Even the childhood memory of them riveled anything he had encountered in his line of work. Kevin was pretty sure he had glimpsed a few items stored on the shelves in the basement. The urgency of the circuit breaker made it impossible for him to explore, but that childhood curiosity and interest in strange oddities held his attention now. No way did he want to leave without finding out what weirdness this box held.

"No," Esmae started.

"No?" Kevin tried not to sound disappointed.

"I mean, no, I don't want to be scared anymore," Esmae looked at Myrtle.

Myrtle reached over and patted Esmae's arm. "Good girl. Never know what fate has in store."

"I'm still unsure about fate," Esmae said.

Myrtle squeezed Esmae's arm, "That will happen

when…well, when fate deems." She smiled and Esmae gave a half smile back.

This solidified an understanding between Myrtle and Esmae that Kevin found cryptic. He realized what secret they kept between them wasn't meant for him, not that it didn't make him more curious about everything.

"Kevin," Myrtle's stare transfixed him. "Shouldn't you be getting home to Julie and the kids?"

A frown kept Kevin from speaking for a moment. "No." Kevin cleared his throat. "Julie is living at her parents' place. The kids are with her tonight."

"Oh, I'm so sorry," Esmae reached out and placed her hand on his arm. "Are you okay? Is everything going to be okay?"

"I'm not sure," Kevin said. "She's seeing someone else. Has been…" His voice broke. Julie was the third person he dated in high school. Esmae married Sparky the summer after their senior year, and Kevin married Julie within a year after that.

A sadness they usually buried around others, surfaced in their eyes as they looked at each other. Kevin placed his hand on top of Esmae's and slid the other underneath, squeezing Esmae's hand in between. He was tempted to fluff her hair to distract from his discomfort, like he had when they were teens sitting on the floor in her bedroom. But, he didn't. Their mutual understanding of pain, betrayal, and rejection bridged the years of separation. They became friends again in that moment.

The tea kettle whistled from the kitchen interrupted the silent connection.

"I think we need tea," Myrtle said quietly. "Kevin, would you be a dear? I need to chat with Esmae."

"No problem, Lady Myrtle," Kevin looked down as his face flushed red with embarrassment. Then he breathed in — chest full, shoulders squared — and breathed out. Kevin knew he didn't have to hide who he was with these two. He looked up and half-smiled at both ladies, squeezed Esmae's hand, then let it slip away as he stood and went to the kitchen to make them all tea. "Earl Grey?" he called back.

"Perfect," Myrtle said loudly enough for him to hear, then spoke softly to Esmae. "Would you like him to stay or go?"

This took Esmae by surprise. Should he not stay? Should he not see what was in the box? "I'm not sure," she said searching Myrtle's face.

"Oh, it doesn't matter," Myrtle said. "Not life or death or anything. I want you to be comfortable."

An image of the black spider Kevin took off her shoulder popped into Esmae's head. She shuddered. "Oh, I think he should stay. The dust and cobwebs on this box means…he should stay and I should go." Esmae chuckled nervously.

"He is a good protector…" Myrtle trailed off in contemplation. "Reminds me of my Earl…" She pulled on the silver chain around her neck, then patted the locket which rested right above her heart.

The Irish narrator chose that moment to say *I know that I shall meet my fate. Somewhere among….* Esmae repeated the words out loud. "I know that I shall meet my fate. Somewhere among…."

"The oddities and curiosities of that box," Kevin finished as he set the tea tray down between them on the table, the cups and saucers rattling together.

The box rattled in response.

Chapter 8

"Welp, this seems like a job for Kevin," Esmae said, as she held a pillow in front of her as protection for what might be in the box. She knew it wasn't much protection, but it did make her feel better.

The box rattled for a few seconds, stopped, then in a few minutes would rattle again. From their positions, each stared into the box waiting to see if something would pop out, if it would continue, or if one of them would have the courage to explore its contents.

Lifting his cup of tea, Kevin sipped it in quiet contemplation.

"Did you get your three sugars?" he looked at Myrtle, who stirred the melting sugar cubes, dispersing their goodness to all layers of her Earl Grey tea.

"Why yes," she lifted her cup to him in a small salute, then sipped. "Thank you." And sipped again.

These pleasantries were a diversion and gave them a few minutes to avoid the task of exploring the box. Except for the rattle of the box, each felt a curiosity and wonderment similar to a child on Christmas morning what was wrapped up and what surprises they might find. What mysteries and oddities it held finally piqued their interest past the point of avoidance.

"I have an idea," Kevin said and disappeared through the bookshelves to the kitchen. A few minutes later he was back with plastic cleaning gloves and a small bucket with warm water and three washcloths. Esmae and Myrtle nodded their agreement as he handed each a pair of gloves.

"We can wash as we go." Kevin set the bucket down and then sat down in the space between the fireplace and the box. He reached up and turned his headlamp on and angled it down and away from the ladies' faces.

Esmae and Myrtle joined him, kneeling across from Kevin and at opposite corners of the box. Once settled, they grabbed the box cover flaps with thickly protected hands and pulled down three sides, fitting them close to the box and held there by their knees.

After Kevin pulled down the box flap on his side, he leaned over, and the lit up the contents of the box with his headlamp, revealing a jumble of indistinguishable items wrapped in ripped newspaper and others wrapped in a variety of materials: leather, velvet, and cloth. A few parts poked through these wrappings, but these peeks did not give a clue to what the whole item might be.

The box rattled again.

No perceptible movement could be detected from the top. With relief, Esmae realized the possibilities it could be an animal were slim, which made her lose her hesitancy about digging into the contents. A memory of a rattle danced in the distant shadows of her mind, but Esmae couldn't grasp the image solidly. Whatever memory the rattle connected to, Esmae figured it must be one of her first memories when she was three or four years old, before her parents died.

A quiet awe fell over the shop as each reached down, lifted an item, then unwrapped it. Only the crackle of the fire and a few "oohs" and "ahs" accompanied their reverent and, otherwise, wordless exploration.

A dusty layer coated the outside wrappings and covered their gloved hands. At first, they tried washing each piece, but the wet only thickened the dirt when they picked up a new piece. With a few movements and quick understanding, they decided to unwrap each piece, throw the wrappings into two separate piles—the newspaper in one and the velvet, leather, and other materials into another. The items were placed on the floor beside them. Esmae wanted desperately to explore each item thoroughly as it was unwrapped, but that didn't seem as efficient as unwrapping them and concentrating on the item after.

Piece after piece, they unwrapped twenty or so until they came to the last two items in the box. Kevin took the larger item and removed the velvet wrapping which revealed a large piece of wood with carved initials.

In the bottom of the box, the last item rattled through a bottom layer of dust-bunnies and perceptively moved through the ragged newspaper. Unmuffled by the many things which had been on top of it, the item clicked, buzzed, and emitted a hollow tin sound. Esmae hesitated, but she wanted to know what this was. She knew this noise. She was sure she had heard it before.

Esmae reached in and took it out, placing it on her lap. Ripping through the newspaper, three mechanical wind-up toys made Esmae express surprise with an "ooooh". These items were considerably old with scratches and worn sides to each.

Poking at them, the cat rattled and moved. Esmae grasped it and lifted it so both Kevin and Myrtle could see the mechanics of the wheels moving underneath. A key fell from the side of the cat and clanked onto the floor. Myrtle picked it up.

"I remember these," she said. "Japan made a number of these rollover clockwork cats at the turn of the century, but I think this one is after 1940. May I?"

Esmae handed her the cat. Myrtle inserted the key and wound the cat up. After removing the key, she placed the cat on the floor. The cat moved forward looking like it was chasing the ball painted in its front paws. The wheels rolled it forward a couple inches, then the larger wheel rolled the cat on its side, over, then over again. Chased the ball, then rolled over again. All the while a loud rattle echoed against the wood floor.

"This is from the 1940s?" Kevin asked. "That's clever. I had no idea they had toys like this back then."

"There were plenty of toys like that," Myrtle said.

Esmae looked down to the other two windup toys. Large enough to cover her hand was a red ladybug with a cartoonish face and dots on its back. She turned the key in the side of the ladybug, and nothing happened. "I hope my tipping the box over didn't break anything," Esmae said.

Within a second, she felt Myrtle pat her arm. "What is meant to be, will be," Myrtle said, and gestured with her hand for the ladybug. Fiddling with the wheels and loosening the internal mechanisms, Myrtle had the ladybug swiftly rolling toward the fireplace within a few seconds. Kevin caught it and turned it back toward Myrtle.

The next windup toy was a rabbit with a faded four-leaf clover painted on its underbelly. This, too, was distressed with age, but when Esmae carefully wound it up, the rabbit hopped the few feet to Myrtle with slow, precise vigor.

"Don't you find it interesting that the rabbit has a four-leaf clover on its belly?" Esmae asked Myrtle, who picked the rabbit up and examined it more closely.

"Yeah, that clover isn't part of the original," Myrtle said thoughtfully.

"Four leaf clovers and rabbits are symbols of good luck in Ireland," Kevin offered.

"Ha," Esmae looked at him in disbelief. "And how would you know that?"

"I read a book on Ireland once," Kevin teasingly said with some pride.

"And do you remember anything else?"

"Nope," Kevin winked at Esmae. "Not at all."

"I didn't unwrap a pen," Myrtle said as she showed what she had unwrapped: an elaborate carved pipe with tobacco stains, two clear dice with another a die inside, two small green and blue sea glass stones, a fork with uneven prongs, a quarter with holes in it, and a journal with dried red, yellow, and white roses and orange, pink, and white lilies pressed between its pages. "This also includes pages written in a language I can't read," Myrtle said as she flipped through the pages. "This might be Gaelic or…a secret language between two lovers. Notice the two hearts drawn in the corners."

She showed Kevin and Esmae the hearts. "Can't help

it," Myrtle said. "I'm a romantic."

Kevin and Esmae didn't believe in love at the moment, so they chose not to respond. Kevin's cynicism made him start to wash off his items, while Esmae reached over and felt the smooth, uneven surface of the sea glass, remarking that it was quite unusual.

"I found some interesting things, too," Esmae said as she looked at the treasures before her and dangled a pocket watch on a chain which had its numbers at the bottom. She shook it and the numbers fell in a haphazard way again to the bottom. Passing it to Simon, Esmae picked up a pen with an intricate marble maze, then a sword letter opener with the small Irish embossment of an embellished four-leaf clover as the ink well. Next was a blue, green, and grey striped pottery coffee mug, then a taller thick, double handled mug with a green oval with a flower in the centre on two sides and decorative lines with a brush inside.

"Oh," Myrtle said with nostalgia, "I haven't seen one of these in ages. This was a shaving mug for the lather." Esmae handed her the mug to feel and reminisce over.

The last items Esmae picked up were unique and piqued her wonderment: a spoon designed with a four-leaf Celtic heart, a twisted piece of driftwood as long and as thick as Esmae's forearm, a scissors in the shape of a stork where its beak formed the scissors and its legs formed into the circular handles, and a pendant with two sets of fingerprints.

Kevin lifted the treasures he had unwrapped. The first was a round, three-player cribbage board. "This has the same four-leaf Celtic symbol as the letter opener and that ink well. Remember when we played cribbage, Izzy?" Kevin handed her the cribbage board.

"I remember beating you at a number of games," Esmae said.

"You think?" Kevin said. "I let you win."

"Yeah, right." Esmae teased back. She flipped the cribbage board over. "This is thick," she said. "There should be…" Esmae trailed off as she felt around the edge until she found a button and pushed it. This allowed the top to be removed, revealing a lid which Esmae slid back. In the drawer underneath, she found circular playing cards and eight pegs for the board.

"See," Esmae showed Kevin the cards. "I'm good at puzzles and beating you."

"Yeah, yeah," Kevin chuckled. "This is cool," he said as he showed them a ship in a cracked bottle. "And took a lot of work." Bits of the sail had broken off, but the pirate flag and other minute details like the gun ports, helm, and rudder were still in tack.

Next, Kevin unrolled a map with pin holes in it over Europe and the United States and then a small piece of wood burnt with jagged lines. "I think this wood has been struck by lightning," Kevin said, rolling it around with his hands. "Fascinating."

"What's the last thing you have over there?" Myrtle asked.

The last item was the heaviest and largest. Kevin lifted a piece of wood cut from a trunk of a tree. The bark framed the smooth interior carved into a heart shaped with the initials P.O. & M.C.

"Awww," Esmae sighed, a lump stuck in her throat. Such a romantic gesture to carve initials in the trunk of a tree for all to see.

Myrtle reached over and squeezed her arm. They gave each other sympathetic smiles.

"I wonder who P.O. and M.C. are," Kevin said.

"The box says Paddy," Esmae said.

"Paddy O'Malley," the name sparked Myrtle's memory. "And Maggie. They had a daughter, Evelyn, and a son… I forget his name. A while back Evelyn moved to Florida. You know, these below-zero Minnesota winters can be hard on the old body."

"You betcha," Esmae said in agreement.

As Kevin looked at all sides of the log, it was rounded with a half-moon on the ends and flat on the backside. When he turned it over, something inside clinked against the sides. Kevin shook it, making it clink repeatedly against the interior.

"There's something inside," Kevin held it up to his ear and shook it in short bursts, the clinking answered with rabid echoes.

Exploring the sides and ends of this wooden box closely, Kevin noticed the roughness of the bark hid two lines two inches apart. They stretched end to end through the middle of the log. The lines followed the natural flow of the bark, to make them harder to detect.

"There's a compartment here…" Kevin said as he flipped and inspected different areas on the wood chunk. "I don't know how to open it."

Esmae observed as Kevin examined the log more. Puzzles intrigued her and this box was full of them. The pen maze, the hard to access compartment of the cribbage board, the ship in the bottle—which wasn't a secret but still took ingenuity and the ability to put together a puzzle, the pendant with the fingerprints was a mystery, the pocket watch with broken numbers—why would someone keep such a piece, and the journal not only included dried flowers but words in a language no one could read. All of these gave insight into Paddy and Maggie's love of puzzles and mystery.

"Would you mind if I tried?" Esmae said.

Kevin poked around the bottom a few more times, then gave the wood to Esmae.

The roughness of the bark scratched her hands, but the bottom and top were smooth.

"Almost like they wanted to throw a person off," Esmae mused. The fire threw shadows on the box making it difficult for Esmae to see any subtle differences. After pressing in some of the same places Kevin had, Esmae thought of something else.

"Kev, let me use your flashlight."

A second later Esmae held the log upright on its end with the initials facing her. She leaned over and shined the light straight down the sides of the log. This allowed her to clear the shadows and see any imperfections. There were none.

"I could always take it back to the shop and saw it open," Kevin suggested with a shrug of his shoulders. "That would make quick work of it."

"Yeaaah," Esmae said, reluctantly agreeing with him. "But then it might destroy whatever is inside. And, if they hid it so well, there has to be something special in there."

"True," Myrtle said as she dried off the soap and water from the last of her items. "And what if it is some sort of metal that ruins your machine. We wouldn't want that to happen either."

Kevin hadn't thought of that. "These are definitely curiosities and oddities, Myrtle, and belong in your shop. I wonder why you didn't have them out."

"When Earl was alive," Myrtle said as she washed a few items Esmae had taken from the box, "we consistently received donations from several estates. Some ended downstairs and I lost track of them. We don't get them as frequently now since there's a Goodwill down the road.

"Of course, they don't take the real unusual and exotic." Myrtle motioned to the stuffed owl looking down at them from the top of a nearby bookshelf. They looked and the fire made the owl's glass eyes glow and seemingly glare at them, making them both shudder. They looked at each other and chuckled, acknowledging their mutual feeling of being unsettled.

"I call that one Earl," Myrtle continued. "Because I feel protected knowing he's looking down on me."

Kevin and Esmae looked at each other again and shook their heads. Nope, that wasn't how they felt.

Esmae picked up the log by its ends and started to hand it back to Kevin, when it twisted, making Kevin's headlamp highlight small cuts Esmae hadn't seen before.

"Wait," she said, taking it back. Esmae laid the log flat side down on her lap and felt along the back.

She couldn't feel or see a thing. But she knew it was there. Her heart pounded. She was one step closer to getting this puzzle solved.

This excitement, she realized, was keeping her from being able to feel the subtle changes in the wood.

"Want me to…" Kevin started.

"Wait…," Esmae said again, then half-smiled an apology at Kevin. "Give me a sec."

Taking a deep breath, then another, then another, allowed Esmae's heart to slowdown. When she felt relaxed, she closed her eyes and, with deliberate gentleness, she moved her fingers along the bottom line of the bark. Then back again even more unhurriedly. There, she felt it, a hairline indentation, bark, then another slight indentation. She moved her fingers back to the middle and pushed in at the bark. An inconspicuous click released the bottom of the log and Esmae lifted the larger piece away from the detached bottom.

The heavier piece gone, the bottom wood panel's invisible hinge slipped out of the other side allowing a silver skeleton key to fall out of the compartment and onto her lap. Esmae flipped the log over, setting the initial side down on the floor, and picked up the key. An old-fashioned skeleton key with a long neck, two prongs at one end, and, at the other end as the handle, the outline of the four-leaf clover heart symbol.

"They sure liked that four-leaf clover, didn't they?" Kevin said. "They used it in so many things, even the letter opener."

"Nothing is ever what it seems," Myrtle said. "What do you think, Esmae?"

"I agree," Esmae turned the key over and over in her hand. "They hid this in a secret compartment, why?"

Kevin reached over, picked up the larger piece, and shook it. There was no noise this time. "But this didn't open the middle compartment," Kevin said, pointing at the two lines faintly seen in the middle of the log.

"Myrtle," Esmae said. "This is an older house, right?"

"Yep, build in 1915," Myrtle said.

"Did you ever use a skeleton key…?" Esmae started, then stopped. "No, never mind. Why would this skeleton key work in a door? If it's found in this piece of wood, it should open this piece of wood…somehow." Esmae's head hurt. She held both ends of the key and rolled it around, accidentally twisting the ends.

The handle end of the key moved in one direction and the prongs moved in another. Loosened, Esmae pulled them apart. A five-inch needle slipped out of the long key and prongs, like a steel sword coming out of an aged iron sheath. The four-leaf clover heart became the sword's hilt.

"It's a needle," Esmae held it up and the silver steel glinted from the firelight.

"So, that part," Kevin scratched his head and looked at the piece of wood in his hands. "That needle part is supposed to unlock another part in this log? Another secret compartment?"

"I think so."

"Okay," Kevin shook his head, looking around for a lamp to move closer. "Okay. We need more light." He put down the log and stood up.

"And I think we need water and a little break," Myrtle said. "Maybe clean up a little? Right, Kevin?"

Kevin hesitated. His focused determination was on opening the puzzle box, but he could never refuse Myrtle. Without exuding the tinge of frustration he felt, Kevin started to gather up the dusty newspaper. He crumpled all of it into a manageable size.

"Sure, sure…" Esmae absentmindedly said to both as she contemplated how and where the needle might possibly fit into the log. If it was like the last lock, the next piece would be released with a click, but being so thin, it could be impossible to find.

"May I have the log?" Esmae asked.

Kevin threw the newspaper into the fire, roaring the flames to life instantly. The fire's heat blazed a toasty warmth and light on all three of them. With his hands free, Kevin picked up the log and handed it to Esmae.

As Esmae looked at the log, Kevin and Myrtle picked up the leather and velvet wrappings, rags, pail of dirty water, and tea tray. Kevin carried the bulk of them to the kitchen.

This intrigue, this brain game, this figuring the puzzle

out felt good to Esmae. She had forgotten how much she enjoyed the challenge and the accomplishment of solving mysteries.

While being methodical and meticulous, Esmae slowly examined and felt each inch of the piece of wood. First the underside where the panel had been removed. This revealed another solid piece of wood. There were no needle-like holes. Next Esmae explored the ends, beyond the faint lines indicating another compartment, there were no needle-like holes there either.

Esmae had explored the bark frame before, but now she did so with even more precision, wishing she had a magnifying glass. Any fold, any rough patch of bark, any shadow could hold a needle-like hole. She took Kevin's flashlight and shined all shadows away.

After intense search of the bark, Esmae needed to release the tension in her neck. She stretched her neck shoulder to shoulder, then side to side. She used her hand to push her neck even further to the right, cracking it. Next, she pushed her neck further to the left, pushing, stretching, and cracking it. Still needing to release more tension, Esmae stood, leaned forward, touching her hands down to her feet, cracking her back. Then she stretched her back by putting pressure on her buttocks and twisting her spine the opposite way, and she did the other side.

From the kitchen, the teakettle's whistle and Myrtle's

laughter floated to Esmae. Determined to figure this puzzle out, Esmae sat back down and held the piece of wood in her hands. Such love and care had gone into its creation. The artful carving of the heart, the initials…Esmae looked at them closer. Small hearts were carved into the dots between the initials.

That seemed out of place to Esmae. Taking her finger, she felt along the initials. P and O and M and C. Each had a depth to it, which took time. She felt the dots between each initial and shined a light on them. The shadow didn't leave. Each dot, Esmae realized, had been burrowed down, but was so thin the burrowing was imperceptible.

Esmae took the sword needle and pushed it into the heart dot after the initial P. The needle went down a few inches, but stopped and stuck into the wood. Esmae felt the needle stick and, with effort, pulled the needle out

Carefully, Esmae pushed the needle into the dot after the O, then the M. Again, the needle went down a few inches, but Esmae made sure to stop when it hit solid wood so it wouldn't stick like it had the first time.

Lastly, Esmae pushed the needle into the dot after the C, expecting the needle to stop a few inches in. This time it did not. The needle kept going until almost the whole needle was in the hole.

Pushing deeper, the needle didn't stick into the wood but hit something smooth and metal. That's when Esmae heard a click, and her heart skipped a beat. She had found the lock to the secret compartment.

With gentle care, Esmae opened the top of the log exposing a compartment filled with a stack of pictures, a wooden spoon, a sealed envelope, and, underneath these things, a dark purple velvet cloth. A feeling of destiny made Esmae's hands shake as she first touched it and removed it from the compartment.

The solid, exact build of the puzzle box had kept the velvet cloth from fading or being aged. Its smoothness felt luxurious and lavish to Esmae, a richness which hinted at something precious.

She unfolded another layer, enjoying the feel, then peeled back another and another layer. The next layer revealed a green feather with a colorful oblong eye with an outline of light green framing a thicker tan and constructing a shadow to the dark blue pupil and light blue iris. Esmae recognized it as a peacock feather.

Pulling back the rest of the layer, another peacock feather was revealed. Both feathers were secured together by a five-inch silver, ornamental metal grip, at the end it held a thin metal pen tip.

Is this the pen that goes with the ink well? Esmae thought. She picked it up by the ornate grip, her fingers fitting perfectly into the worn, smooth grooves.

Esmae grabbed the ink well, took off its lid, and stuck

the pen in. The ink at the end of the pen began to glow and drip on to the table. Quickly, Esmae took a napkin and wiped up the ink. The pen's tip still glowed.

With her focus completely on the pen, Esmae hadn't heard the footsteps behind her coming closer.

"Woah," Kevin said, making her jump with surprise. "What's going on, Izzy? How are you doing that?"

Chapter 9

"We made sandwiches," Myrtle said as she walked in with a jug of cold tea and motioned to the tray of turkey sandwiches Kevin carried in. "We used real Kraft mayo instead of Miracle Whip and…" She stopped in midsentence.

Esmae held the glowing pen up so Myrtle could see it. Kevin stared with a slightly open mouth, wide eyes, and silence.

Myrtle looked at the glowing pen and then at the look of surprise on Kevin's face. "Well, guess the cat is out of the bag," Myrtle said putting down the jug of tea and glasses. "I wonder…" and she held out her hand for the pen.

When Esmae placed it in Myrtle's hand, the pen immediately stopped glowing. Myrtle handed it to Kevin, who put the tray down on the table, and took the pen. The feathers waved as he investigated it from all sides, then he shook it. Nothing rattled, but the feathers flopped frantically back and forth.

Putting a hand on his hand, Myrtle stopped him. "I think these feathers might be a tad bit delicate and fragile for that." She took the pen from him and handed it back to Esmae, where it instantly glowed again.

"Cool" was Kevin's stunned response. "But, how?" Then he laughed awkwardly. "This is a magic trick, isn't it, Izzy?"

"No…," Esmae said. As much as she wanted to lie, she didn't. "We don't know."

Myrtle pooh-poohed that answer a bit in a teasing way as she separated the glasses and poured some peach tea into each. "She's humble," Myrtle said. "I believe it's because Esmae has tapu, or deep spiritual connection and destiny to this pen and to the ink well."

Esmae picked up the open bottle and the ink inside the well began to glow more brilliantly, answering Kevin's questioning expression.

"Understood," he said in amazement.

Kevin placed a sandwich on a paper plate and sat on the couch watching the ink well glow in Esmae's hand.

"Did this happen the other day?"

Esmae explained how dark it had been down in the basement, how scared she had been, how Paddy's box dropped, and the ink well glowed so she could find her way out.

"But no pen would work with this ink," Esmae

continued. "And that's why we wanted to go through the box."

Myrtle produced a piece of blank notepaper and placed it on the table. Her grey eyes lit up with anticipation as she smiled at Esmae encouragingly. "Go ahead, see if it will work now."

Esmae put the ink well down on the table and carefully held the pen by its grip. After taking one more look at Kevin and Myrtle, she lifted the pen up and dipped it into the ink well. The ink on the pen and the ink in the well glowed brightly when she contacted either one or both at the same time, depending on if the pen she held made contact with the ink inside or not. She wiped the excess ink off the pen by sliding it across the top of the ink well, and lightly pressed the pen tip to paper.

The ink created no image. The ink seemed to disappear into the page.

Esmae tried pressing the pen tip harder into the paper. Nothing showed up.

She dipped the pen again, not wiping off the excess ink this time. Again, nothing showed up. She hit the tip gently on the paper. The ink splattered on the page, even the splotches faded quickly.

The paper and ink seemed to repel each other.

"Maybe it's invisible ink?" Kevin suggested. Standing up, he walked over and lit his lighter, then leaned over holding the flame close to the paper, being careful not to hold it too close so it wouldn't catch on fire, but close enough that the heat from the lighter would activate anything in the ink.

Still, nothing.

"What about vinegar?" Myrtle suggested. She hurried into the kitchen and was back within a few minutes with a bottle of white vinegar and a few cotton balls. She soaked a cotton ball with vinegar and dabbed the paper with it. Nothing showed up.

"Curiouser and curiouser, said Alice," Esmae and Kevin said at the same time. Looking at each other, they laughed. This was one of the quotes they used when they were teens.

"Jinx," Esmae said.

"Perfect," Kevin's deep, hearty laugh dissipated the tension and focused seriousness.

As they ate, they talked about the other items in the box. They bemused their significance and why the family donated these strange, but obviously personal, items. Questions like these didn't have an immediate answer.

"And the wood puzzle seems like it would be a family heirloom. Or even…," Esmae leaned over and picked up the pictures and letter from the secret compartment, "…these seem incredibly sentimental." She passed them to Myrtle who passed them to Kevin.

The first black and white picture was faded, with scratches and small patches etched off in the corners and along the side and bottom edges, where it had been held countless times. The unsmiling faces of a young couple were blurry but distinguishable as they stood in front of a stone wall with rolling hills and sheep in the background. On the back written in faded ink and in slanted cursive were the words: *Paddy & Maeve, married Galway, Ireland 1894.* The next pictures showed a growing family. In one, the couple held a baby with *Pennsylvania 1895* written on the back. Another showed the couple with an older boy and another baby, on the back: *Martin, age 9 and Evelyn, 1905, Detroit Lakes, MN.*

A colorized picture displayed the couple with wrinkles but smiling, looking adoringly at each other. An auburn red streaked through Maeve's hair, the blue in the sky was faded, as were the yellow and red roses in Maeve's bouquet. The back read: *Paddy & Maeve, 30th anniversary, 1924.*

Esmae passed Myrtle the last photograph showing Maeve surrounded by three or four couples and many children at various ages. Paddy was nowhere in the picture. Maeve's smile bespoke pride, and her arms embraced as many of the smaller children as she could. This was the clearest picture and the inscription on the

read: *O'Malley family clan at Grania's 95th birthday, 1961.*
Maeve's red hair had gone completely white, but her
smile hadn't changed from the first picture to the last.

"Why Grania?" Kevin asked when he read the back of
the picture.

"Right?" Esmae agreed, wondering why. "Is that how
they say 'grandma' in Irish?"

"No," Myrtle said. "Grania was an Irish woman pirate
back in the sixteenth century. I have a book on her
history...somewhere...I think back in that corner area."
Myrtle pointed to the back of the shop opposite to the
bathroom and door to the basement.

"A lady pirate," Kevin said. "That's cool. Flowing red
hair? Probably a stubborn temper..."

"Hey, now," Esmae swatted at him.

Kevin put up his hands in protest. "I'm just saying,
she'd have to be stubborn to be a pirate with a bunch of
men. And having a temper wouldn't hurt either."

"He's right," Myrtle said. "From what I've read, she
was beyond remarkable."

"Hmmm, someone I need to read more about," Esmae
said. Then picked up the yellowed envelope with
flourished script on the front. "This is addressed to
Grania? I can't read what these words are." She passed it
to Myrtle.

"*Mo shíorghrá* or muh HEER ggrawh," Myrtle said, "is

Gaelic for 'my eternal love'."

"Awww," a lump caught in Esmae's throat and her heart ached. Esmae swallowed hard in frustration at herself and ignored these internal, emotional signs. There was no reason romantic words should produce such an unsolicited response. "What does the rest of the letter say?"

"But…*should* we read it?" Kevin asked. "Exploring the pictures, dissecting the box. All of this," he waved his hands at all the objects, "already seems like we've intruded on their private lives."

Myrtle hesitated before setting the envelope down on the table. "I suppose you're right."

They sat there in silence, looking at the envelope, trying to decide if reading it was the right thing to do.

"What about that other item," Kevin said, getting up and going over to the pile. He picked up the spoon and brought it back to the table to examine it.

"Okay, wow, the time and energy put into creating this spoon," he said. "Look, these links and the spoon itself is carved out of one piece of wood. That's extremely hard to do." He held up the spoon and showed them the intricate details. The chain of five links at the top of a heart created by Celtic knotwork which branched off into two hearts, one with a lock hole carved in the middle and the other carved with the outline of a key into its center. These hearts came together and twisted into the stem of the spoon, then ended with the head of a spoon.

"A Welsh love spoon," Myrtle said.

"Welsh?" Kevin said. "Isn't that English...like from England? Haven't the Irish hated the English, for centuries? Why would an English love spoon be in an Irish family heritage box?"

"The letter might give us some clues," Esmae offered, shrugging her shoulders, trying to be nonchalant.

"Nice try, sweetie," Myrtle said, her eyes twinkled.

"Well, Myrtle," Esmae said. "Seems to me, this box has either been in your possession since 1961 or 1972 when Evelyn moved to Florida. Either way, ten or twenty years, don't think we're infringing too much." She looked at Kevin apologetically. "Sorry. I do agree, it does seem personal and private," she paused before continuing. "But aren't you curious?" Esmae picked up the ink well, which glowed instantly. "Don't you want to know why this glows for me and no one else?"

"The letter might hold clues," Myrtle said, picking up the letter. The bell twinkled as the door creaked open interrupting the conversation.

"Hey, cry baby," a voice called. "Are you here? Albert wants to spend time with you."

Esmae felt deflated. "I don't think he should see this stuff, definitely not the ink well."

"We've got this," Kevin said. "You go and we'll take care of this."

"Thank you," Esmae said, looking at them both with a weak smile and gratefulness in her heart. "Coming," she said louder, so Sparky could hear, and she hurried to catch him by the front display tables so he wouldn't see the treasures of the box…or Kevin.

Chapter 10

The evening with Albert and Sparky went better in ways Esmae never expected or planned. Albert wanted to fish on the pontoon one last time before taking the boat in for winter. Esmae didn't want to spend time with Sparky, but her love for her youngest son humbled her. What she found was that a day of figuring out puzzles, of being creatively productive, of finding treasures, and of being found special—she was the only one the ink and pen glowed for—had a way of calming her so Sparky's attempt at teasing her and pushing her buttons didn't bother her. His attempts at irritations and annoyances flowed off her like water on a duck's back.

When Sparky realized his goading wasn't getting to Esmae, he talked about other things and brought out the beer, allowing Albert to have one, indirectly daring Esmae to say something and start a fight. In front of Albert, Esmae would look like the bad guy, the mean mom, the uncool parent. Esmae didn't like boating and drinking at the same time, and Sparky knew this. But, Esmae didn't say anything. She positioned herself to drive, which Sparky couldn't deny. Drinking and driving a boat was legal in Minnesota, as long as no one was intoxicated. She wasn't going to chance her or Albert's lives. Not Sparky's either.

They fished, talked, and played cards.

Albert gave her a huge hug when they dropped her off back at the shoppe. The sincerity behind his "Thanks, Mom," touched her heart and made her yearn for the way things had been. She hoped one day Albert would understand why days like today didn't happen as often as they did before—and not blame her.

"The best revenge is a life well lived." This had been Myrtle's advice when Esmae said she wasn't sure what life had in store or if she was meant to stay with Sparky. When they first started dating, life seemed like it was meant to be, like they were destined to be together.

Now, she didn't believe in destiny. Life was about choices and trying to figure out what a 'life well-lived' meant to her.

Esmae scribbled a quick note to herself. *This does not mean what my life would look like to make Sparky jealous. That would make living my life about him and not for myself. So...what would a successful life look like to me, not compared to anyone else?*

Esmae had no clue.

What she did know, she wanted to figure out the intrigue of the glowing ink pen and well. Then she would see what she wanted for her future. Kismet and Sparky be damned. Her choices would be for her not for destiny, not for fate, and definitely not about making Sparky happy or jealous.

The last word reverberated in Esmae's heart, making her not want to admit the feelings it conjured up, making her feel torn and internally divided.

Esmae knew, making her almost-ex feel jealous would require her to seek revenge.

She couldn't do that.

She believed in karma. She was Minnesota nice. And God's word said, "Vengeance is mine sayeth the Lord."

But, what if…? Esmae covered her smile with her hand as she thought of how delicious it would be to, at the very least, show Sparky a reflection of himself.

No. Esmae battled the thoughts within. *Forgiveness was key to not seeking revenge.* That was what she had been taught. To forgive meant healing.

She would focus on what would make her life happy, successful, and fulfilled.

Well, at least she would try.

Chapter 11

Dusk created jagged and distorted shadows on the shop's walls. Esmae found this time to be peaceful and was fascinated with the shadows as they lent themselves to a benign eeriness, a crack into a world that might have been, even a world happening now beyond the sight of humans.

The influx of more customers then usual had kept her mind occupied throughout the day. But now, without Myrtle, who went to visit a friend for supper, and Kevin, who was on duty at the firehouse, Esmae felt alone among the shadows. Except for restaurants and gas, most businesses in Detroit Lakes closed at 6 p.m. on a Friday. Myrtle's shop was off the main street of Washington Avenue, which started from the train tracks north of Washington Square Mall, travelled down the center of town, and ended at the southern end by Detroit Lake, the town's namesake.

At 7 p.m., the time and the emptiness of the shoppe, except for the growing shadows, meant Esmae could lock up and go home. Then she would be by herself in another empty space. Esmae shook her head.

Being here would be better than going home, Esmae decided. There was comfort in knowing people were close by who might stop in despite it being a Friday night.

Esmae stared out toward the main drag and remembered a time when she loved cruising with friends down Washington Avenue, checking out everyone, then doing the turnabout at the resort and cruising back up Washington to find a party.

Those were good times, Esmae sighed with a slight smile of melancholy. There was something about living decades with someone and having a shared experience.

Sparky would drive his beat-up Chevy pickup with Esmae by his side while their friends sat in the back bed of the truck on blankets and pillows. They held hands and watched as their friends tried to hook up with the cute shoob they waved at when they cruised by the first time.

At Zorbaz, they ate pizza while laughing and gossiping about the shoobs or planning the next keg party. Shoob was what locals called outsiders or tourists because they usually wore shoes on the beach and either had no tan or were burnt a bright lobster red from the sun. Locals never wore shoes on the beach, much less anywhere else, and had impeccable tan lines. Baby oil, laying out on the beach or in a boat constantly flipping like a frying fish, and doing water sports all summer was the recipe for a perfect baby-brown-bear tan.

Cruising and meeting strangers with the potential to be more, that is what people wanted to do on a Friday night, Esmae admitted. Not spend time perusing a bookstore. And tomorrow, there was a dance at the Pavilion, a weekly occurrence during the summer that happened only on special occasions during the fall and winter seasons.

Weekends during the summer, cruising down Washington, and the huge July Fourth celebration was why USA Today rated Detroit Lakes the best place to visit in the Midwest during the summer, next to Fort Lauderdale on the East Coast and Santa Barbara on the West Coast. Detroit Lakes was home to ten thousand people and couldn't compete with those cities during the winter. But during the summer months, visitors grew D.L. by five to ten times its population. People from all providences of Canada to the Twin Cities to parts unknown came to this small town to find fun, to do water sports, to boat, to golf, to drink, to party, and, subsequently, get laid.

Townies knew they lived in the perfect size. Everyone knew everyone, but could get lost if need be. That's how it was with Kevin. They dated as teenagers and when they broke up, they went their separate ways. They had crossed paths at the store or bank, and had heard gossip about the other's life; but hadn't had a true, meaningful conversation in decades. Not until the storm fried the circuit breaker.

Time, heartbreak, and treasure findings made them friends again.

Esmae absentmindedly twirled and tightened a curl of hair draped around her face with her finger, then untightened it. Kevin wasn't her future. He couldn't be. His friendship, full of teasing and understanding, felt familiar, like a brother. What they had decades ago was in the past, they couldn't go back. Esmae twisted the curl tight into her finger as she wondered if he felt the same way.

I'll probably never love again, Esmae thought. She waited to see if the Irish narrator contradicted her. Except for a few headlights shining through the windows, growing the shadowy distortions on the walls and ceiling until they suddenly shrunk as the car passed, no other movement or sound interrupted Esmae's thoughts.

Esmae stood up and deeply inhaled the peace and loneliness, simultaneously comforting and solemn. This would be how she would spend her days until her death. Being at peace with oddities and dying with a bunch of cats. Esmae recalled her inner Irish voice once telling her otherwise.

Hmmmm, did he mean it? Esmae wondered if inner voices could be wrong, because if she wasn't with Sparky her life's trajectory was on the path of a cat lady. Shaking the idea off, she walked to the kitchen to make Irish Breakfast tea and grab a turkey-cucumber sandwich, then she switched off more of the lights and sat by the fire to eat. An hour to enjoy the shadows and the firelight keeping the shadows from totally engulfing her.

Curiosity was no stranger to her.

The Irish narrator was back, his voice an unexpected and loud intrusion into the quiet crackle of the fire and darkening shadows. *The letter held secrets she not only wanted, but should know.*

Esmae looked around, her brows furrowed and her lips pressed into a grimace. Most of the time the voice had an uncanny accuracy to what she was thinking in the moment. This time, well, the letter hadn't been on her mind. Thoughts of traveling to see her older children and how life hadn't turned out as she planned had danced in her head until the voice interrupted, not like a gentleman with a gentle tap on her shoulder, but as a loud, burly partner with two left feet.

Of course, she knew exactly which letter the voice referred to. Esmae paused as she looked around, trying to spy the letter among the shadows.

"Now that the narrator mentioned it," Esmae spoke out loud. Her voice sounding loud in the silence, "Where is that letter? Where did you put it, Myrtle?"

A white light started as a faint glow from the mantel. The longer Esmae did not see it, the brighter it became and contrasted through the golden flames of the fire as a beacon. Esmae walked hesitantly toward it, her eyes adjusting with each step. Before she couldn't see it because of the assortment of knick-knacks on the mantel as well as it being hidden in the shadows behind the ink well and pen. Now the ink well illuminated the letter.

Carefully removing the ink well with one hand, Esmae gently took the letter with the other. She brought them back to the chair and placed the ink well on the table, which continued to illuminate like a lantern when Esmae removed her touch. This allowed Esmae to read the front of the envelope again, *Mo shíorghrá*, to his 'eternal love'. Esmae traced her fingers over the ink. They did not glow. She flipped the envelope over and as her fingers held the bottom of the envelope, an intricate inked symbol of the key with the four-leaf heart and cross illuminated.

This was a sign, Esmae decided as she fingered the key. Where she touched, the ink brightened slightly. *This has to be a sign that I'm meant to read this letter.* Esmae's heart pounded and twisted with indecision. She shouldn't because Kevin could be right. Reading an intimate letter was an infringement into Paddy and Maeve's privacy. Their daughter probably didn't understand what she had given away.

But he could be wrong, Esmae reasoned. The ink well continued to glow without her touch. *There must be a reason*. She touched the far edge of the envelope's flap. It did not easily pull away from back of the envelope. *Maybe the letter hasn't been opened before…* Esmae wondered if Paddy hid the letter so completely that Maeve had never found or read it.

The ink well's light brighten when she heard her inner Irish narrator state: *There was no denying, she was meant to read the letter.*

This knotted Esmae up inside even more with indecision. She shook her head and tried to reason with herself. *My desire to read the letter influenced what he said.*

Esmae rolled her eyes as she quickly contradicted that thought. *Like that had ever happened before,* she shook her head. The Irish narrator exhibited a voice and thoughts of his own, even if it was inside her own head. *Walter Mitty turned out to be a highly creative genius.* Esmae smiled, remembering that old short story her grandmother had read to her. *I'm no genius, but I am a puzzler.* Esmae felt a surge of esteem when giving herself credit where credit was due. *I can figure a moral dilemma out. If the letter can't be opened without forcibly ripping it open with a letter opener, I won't read it.*

With a tender touch, Esmae felt along the edge of the fold and played with the edges. She continued to flip along the edges with her fingers, trying to see if anything was loose. Finding nothing, Esmae sighed with resignation. The letter was sealed. She wouldn't be reading it tonight. With a touch of sadness, Esmae caressed the back of the letter in a random pattern with her fingertips.

As they grazed the middle of the upper fold, a dot, invisible to the naked eye, shined when she touched it. Esmae moved her fingers to the left. More bits and pieces, of what could only be letters, became visible as Esmae's fingers brushed over them. The large capital letters were faint. Age had weathered them and broken the lines so they couldn't illuminate all at once.

Placing the envelope on the table, Esmae held its edge tightly with one hand and moved two fingers around to find the beginning and the end of the letters. With four dots with partial letters in between, Esmae determined there were probably four letters. But how to figure out what the letters were.

Pouring ink on the envelope would ruin what was left of the letters, and likely soak the letter inside. She could try and trace the letters with a pen, but that didn't seem like it would work either.

As Esmae pondered options, she continued to gently rub her finger over the top of the worn letters. Small sections were visible when touched and instantly not when she wasn't touching them.

Almost subconsciously, Esmae moved her fingers quickly side to side over the first letter. The quickness allowed only a slight curve to show in this direction. She moved it quickly up and down in small movements than with larger movements when she realized how big the letter had been written.

"Ah," Esmae said with satisfaction. The first letter was an 'S' and a dot. Doing the same motion on the second letter revealed a 'W' and a dot. Then an 'A' dot 'K' dot.

S.W.A.K.

"Swak?" Esmae tried the word out loud. With dots, meant it was an acronym. "S.W.AAA.K. Swwwak. Shhhhwack. Hmmmm…." Esmae played with the pronunciation, seeing if it jogged her memory. What would an almost eighty-year-old man mean by using S.W.A.K.?

Esmae continued moving her fingers over the letters, then around the letters. Above the letters, a set of invisible lips appeared when she traced over them.

Love, lips, kissing, and a sealed letter. A kissing sound of *mwah* came from her inner Irish narrator. She must be on the right track.

His deep Irish voice began singing:

Tho we gotta say goodbye for the summer
Darling I promise you this

Esmae began humming along to the slow, melodic tune.
The words seemed familiar. She closed her eyes and
listened closer.

I'll send you all my love every day in a letter

Esmae joined him on the last line.

Sealed with a kiss

The next verse they sang together. The words bringing
the wistful feeling of summers ending and the lively
entertainment of seeing Bryan Hyland in concert during
the 60s.

Yes, it's gonna be a cold lonely summer
But I'll fill the emptiness
I'll send you all my dreams every day in a letter
Sealed with a kiss

They hummed the tune and sang "sealed with a kiss"
after words they didn't know.

"Sealed with a kiss. Awww," Esmae couldn't help
letting her heart melt a bit at the thought of an elderly man
leaving a letter for his wife which he 'sealed with a kiss'.
Esmae had never received one, even in her days before
Sparky.

"If this is sealed with a kiss," she tilted the envelope
back and forth, determining how tight the seal was and if

what she was going to do next would work. "Maybe…?" Lifting up the S.W.A.K. part to her lips, Esmae kissed the envelope with a loud "mwah", thinking the sound might help.

There were no streams of bright iridescent light or Hallelujah chorus, but the released fold indicated the seal had been broken. Esmae tried to contain her excitement. Her hands shook, so she put the letter down and got up. Esmae paced nervously back and forth in front of the fireplace, looking at the letter with the ink well's gleam creating a narrow but distinct shadow at the gap between the fold and the envelope.

Rubbing her hands on her jeans, she sat back down and pressed back the fold the rest of the way open then slid the letter from its resting place. The paper was as yellowed and aged as the envelope. In the middle of the page, black spots had soaked through and fingerprints decorated the backside haphazardly with three prints along the middle edge, one in the corner, and two on the opposite corner. Esmae marveled at knowing Paddy, and probably Maeve, too, held the letter in these spots. They forever marked a connection and a sacred testament to Paddy and Maeve's life and that their love continued to exist beyond their lifetime.

Esmae swallowed hard and her chin quivered as she closed her eyes. Tears ran down her cheeks. With a shaky breath, Esmae sniffled and wiped the tears away. Esmae didn't know why, maybe it was the empathic romantic in her, but she felt the pull of love these two shared. With another deep, shaky breath, Esmae accepted her own limitations. Destiny, even fate and faith, were easier to believe in when it was about someone else's life.

Touching the ink spots and fingerprints, Esmae noticed none of them glowed.

"He must have used different ink," Esmae surmised and opened the pages which were folded in half. The letter began with the date in the righthand corner.

September 7, 1934

Dearest Maeve - *macushla*,

You are my own Grania, the pirate of my heart, the one who calms the rough seas of life with a few soft words and a gentle touch. With the heaviest of hearts, I write this to you. The tuberculosis has gotten the better of me and the doctor gives me only a few more months, if not weeks, to live. The hardest part in all of this is not the dying, but in the not living with you.

With a grateful heart, I look back on the good life we've had. Completely unexpected and yet the fates and fairies knew we were destined to be together.

I think you knew because of your papa and maman.

An Englishman and a French woman, across oceans, over a number of years, and through conflict, they came together, all because of two books. Your maman finding it in Verona, Italia and your papa being called to it in Ireland. Thankful he decided to leave his copy in Ireland and your maman kept hers, hoping it called to one of their children.

You, their mon cœur, were chosen by the book. Your younger sisters finding love much easier and sooner than you. You, a bonnie devil-may-care lass, never thinking you would find it, especially not with an Irish sheepherder.

We weren't each other's cup of tea. Had we met in person, we'd have never given each other a second glance. I thought you a bit proper when first we met. If not for the books, I'd not known it was all a façade. You were my cheeky lass, my *cailín*. You may have grown up in England and France, but 'tis the luck of the Irish you were born in Dublin when your papa was returning the book to the Hodges Figgis, the oldest bookstore. In the many a time my pa and I wander through its shelves, as did he with his maimeó and daideó since 1768, I felt the magic always. 'Twas my favorite spot.

It became even more magical when I was called to the book when I started working there when I was about 38. The journey to find the book was filled with obstacles. At times, I wanted to give up. Who knew what was at the end. Alas, when the fairies and the good people finally assisted, I found my way and let fate direct my path, it led us to each other.

My brother couldn't believe what a bleeding heart I'd become, a romantic sap. I sang in pubs for the first time, my heart bursting with love for ye.

Even before we met, I carved our names into that oak on the family farm. If ye noticed, that's what this treasure box is made from. Glad my brother took the time to chop it out after the lightening split it in two.

Our siblings seem to find love in more conventional ways than what we did. Like yours, mine married before me. Surely, I wasn't looking for love, wasn't anything I wanted to deal with. Then your heart called to mine, and I could not resist.

I hope you keep your book, as did your maman. If our grandchildren aren't called, then let it go. As near and dear as it to our story, let destiny reach out and bring together the next pair of loves. That's why I left mine in Ireland. When the time comes, trust the fates and the fables of old, and allow true love's destiny to spread to someone else who needs it, who's lost their way and think they don't deserve love.

Your maman told me once that the owner of the book in Verona said it brought together her and her daughter she had lost during the war. Soulmates do not have to be lovers. Makes me think there must be many types of soulmates out there. For me, there was only you.

How lifeless and unadventurous my life would have been without you. The life we've had, filled with some heartaches and with blessings, too numerous to count.

Our granddaughter reminds me so much of you. Seeing the world's magic beyond the veil and what is possible. My fear is you might lose sight of that during this Crash of '29 and within a few months when I'm gone and can no longer hold you in my arms, you still will be in my heart.

I hope this letter will soothe the storm sure to rage in your heart. As I would rage against God if you were taken from me. Let the rage go knowing we will meet again.

During the last decades, I haven't expressed enough of these thoughts. The time has gone faster then I thought it would. Death came knocking too soon, even at 80. I expected, nere wanted, to live much longer with you, my dearest love.

I implore you, don't give up. Don't lose heart. With the Prohibition over, continue to make your strawberry wine and peach brandy jam. They will be in demand, as subtle as they are. And, our children will need your faith and understanding of the magic and miracles this world can provide.

Wherever you go, whatever you do, I'll see and be so proud of you.

Ye kisses still make me weak in the knees. I shouldn't admit that, but being practically on my death bed I have no more manly ego, if I ever did after reading your letters and responses. They melted the walls around me heart.

I hope the book keeps them, somehow, in the years to come so you can read them. Would be a shame if all the stories of soulmates the books have connected are lost and dinnit encourage the next one to find the ink well, pen, and book. Took me a blasted while to find the only instrument to write to you. When I found it, what joy, my love, to finally respond to you.

Beyond this world, I know there is another. I have the deepest faith because I know, if angels and Tír na nÓg, the Otherworld – with the Lord himself directing it all, the books wouldn't existence, soulmates, such as we, would never find each other. Surely, your parents wouldn't have found each other and you wouldn't exist. Then where would this heart be? Cold and dried up as a mackerel found on the shores of Howth. That be'n the truth.

'Twas Inis Fáil, for Ireland is the Island of Destiny. Ye, I see now how the Irish island is drenched with serendipitous kismet behind every flora and fauna. We were moving toward each other, but would have missed the opportunity if we had met in person first. We would have walked on by. Instead, the first time we met you were an aisling, like a vision or dream to me. I almost dinnit believe you were real.

How grateful I am for your love and the life we've led. You are my soulmate, my eternal love, my heart, my *uisce beatha* – my water of life, more than whiskey could ever be. Life would have been nothing without you.

Your strength and fierceness, your stubbornness and creativity, your love as a wife, mama, and grania, no one could have filled my heart more. And the fates knew it. You're my once in a lifetime.

As the Lord takes me home, I urge you to keep exploring life. Adventure more. Live for both of us and tell me the details when we meet again. For we shall meet again.

My heart breaks a bit, *macushla*, I don't want to leave you. Forgive me. Please know my love stays with you, always and forever.

Your Irish bear,
Paddy

Tears blurred the last words, then trailed down her cheeks. She let them flow even as her conscious tore at her. Reading these intimate words did overstep the bounds of privacy. Kevin was right.

But, they made Esmae's heart ache with romance. Never had she seen a man express such love, mortality, and hope. Men didn't write words like this, not in her experience. Didn't seem possible. But, here they were. This was what true love looked and sounded like.

Esmae wiped the tears away and, with a lump in her throat, read the letter again. The words gripped her so deeply, she didn't hear the cacophony of the bell and door opening and closing.

Chapter 12

"What is this," Sparky pulled the letter away from her, making Esmae jolt and call out in abrupt surprise.

"Hey," The shock of Sparky standing there was overruled by her concern for the letter. "It's nothing." She stood up and tried to snatch it back. "Please…"

"Seems like it's important," Sparky said, holding it high above him, completely out of Esmae's reach. "Especially if you're crying over it. Awww." He sardonically wiped a tear off her cheek. "See," he said with a triumphant, mocking smile, "you are a cry baby." Sparky seemed pleased with himself as he laughed in a way that pained Esmae to her core. She wondered if this was how love would always show up in her life. Not the love Paddy and Maeve showed each other or Myrtle and Earl. Tears of pain fell down her cheeks and she stopped fighting and sat down. With her back to Sparky, she buried her head in her hands to hide the additional tears as they fell.

"Esmae, listen…" Sparky said gently, putting his free

hand on her shoulder. "You know I'm kidding. That's my humor."

"Come now," he said and walked around the table to stand in front of her. "Don't be like that. We have too much history. We have children together."

Esmae didn't look at him but continued to look down and at the shadows from the flames as they danced on his jeans. They distracted her from her pain.

Sparky seemed to realize this and crouched down close to her, putting his hands on her knee to steady himself, the letter crumpling a bit in between his hand and her knee. There was no way to avoid his eyes now, though the light from the ink well had gone out and his features were mostly hidden.

"Esmae," his voice almost pleading, "you know me. You know how much I love you."

"What about what's-her-name?" A flourish of youth, giggles, hair, and perfume came to Esmae's mind.

"That's over," Sparky said and shrugged his shoulder. "When we spent last weekend together with Albert, I realized how much I missed you and wanted you back."

Esmae searched his eyes. The shadows hid them and she could not look deeply enough into them to see if he was telling the truth. Even as he held her gaze, emitting a sense of honesty, disbelief crept in as she thought of how many girlfriends there had been over the years. She had been oblivious until he confirmed the number on Valentine's Day. She thought of all the times she believed him through the years when he had to work late or take a weekend work trip or go to a conference out of state. Thinking about all of those times made her question if she should believe him now.

Though, according to some scientific study Esmae read about in a *New York Times* article, most men who cheat do so out of boredom not because they want to leave. Esmae remembered her grandma saying, "Men want their Kate and Edith, too." Her play on the idiomatic proverb, "People can't have their cake and eat it, too." But not grandpa, she said. Grandpa was one of the good ones.

When they married, Esmae thought Sparky was, too. Then the years drove wedges of hurt, distrust, and disinterest between them. Not like Myrtle and Earl, not like Paddy and Maeve...

"Let me have the letter back," Esmae reached for it, perhaps too quickly because Sparky stood up as quickly and took a couple steps back toward the fire.

Taking another step back, Sparky turned toward the fire, lowering the letter.

"Please," Esmae could barely speak, a lump formed in her throat and heart pounded in her ears as she anticipated the letter being thrown into the fire.

"What's so special about this letter?" Sparky turned

the lowered letter to the fire to be able to read the writing. "Who's Maeve?"

Esmae held her breath as she watched Sparky.

"I can't read this," Sparky waved the letter at her. "This person doesn't write legibly. What does it say?"

The lump in her throat made it difficult to speak.

"Esmae," he insisted. "What made you cry?"

"It's…it's a…," fear gripped her heart, Sparky hated romance. "It's a…love letter."

"A love letter?"

"A very old, antique love letter."

"When was it written?"

"Back in 1934."

"Jeepers. Cool." Sparky exhibited a dubious appreciation of old things. "How much is it worth?"

Esmae frowned. "Nothing. It's a letter."

He waved the letter in her direction. "How much is it worth *to you*?"

Esmae frowned and shook her head not understanding what he meant.

"What is it worth to you?" Sparky repeated. "You're emotional over these few antiquated pages. This made you cry those crocodile tears. How much does that make it worth to you?"

"Sparky," Esmae decided not to play his game. "Please, give it back. It's not even mine, but Myrtle's."

"Hmmm…" Sparky wasn't about to let go of his leverage, even if the letter was Myrtle's property. He took steps toward Esmae and handed her the letter, then snatched it back when she reached for it.

Esmae reached for it again, and Sparky snatched it away, smiling.

"You're too slow," he chuckled.

"Sparky," Esmae said sternly.

"Okay, okay," Sparky said, holding out the letter. Esmae held the other end as Sparky knelt down on one knee in front of her. They both held opposite ends of the letter.

"Come to the dance with me tomorrow."

"The one at the Pavilion?"

"Yes, like we did in the early days," Sparky smiled gently and lovingly, then squeezed her knee with his free hand. "Remember those days? Remember how we used to enjoy dancing?"

Those had been good days, Esmae thought. There had been laughter and friends.

"Please," Sparky said flatly, without meaning. "We can take Albert." These last words had the ring of truth.

A family outing, making memories. Esmae hesitated. Sparky knew the buttons to push to her heart.

"Sure," Esmae said. "As a family."

"Cool," Sparky said, letting go of the letter as he stood

up. He bent over and kissed Esmae on the cheek, then stood back up, completely disregarding the letter like it had been a prop the whole time. "I'll pick you up at, what seven? No, six. We can have dinner together beforehand."

"I'll be here," Esmae said. "I could meet you somewhere."

"Zorbaz," Sparky said, walking around the table, past the tree, the prisms, and the owls. "Let's meet at Zorbaz at five, to miss the crowds. Dance starts at eight, so we could play some miniature golf, too, maybe get ice cream at Dairy Queen." Sparky grew fainter as he walked toward the door. "Love you, Cry Baby." He called back. "See you tomorrow."

An emptiness filled Esmae in her heart and gut, she wasn't sure why.

She held the letter against her chest. "If only...," she said, closing her eyes in a silent yearning for what she was missing. Wishing Sparky was someone she could share the letter with, and knowing he wasn't.

I have nothing more to give you than my heart. The inner Irish voice soothed her yearning and filled the hole in her heart. He continued. *True love is a discipline in which each divines the secret self of the other and refuses to believe in the mere daily self.*

The lump in Esmae's throat and the hole in her heart disappeared, filled with a peaceful acknowledgement and understanding there were people who would care about an old, romantic letter.

She closed her eyes again, smoothing the letter against her chest as she wished on the lights, fairies, and everything connected in the spiritual world, that there was true love and she would find it.

The inner Irish voice echoed her wish.

It is love that I am seeking for,
But of a beautiful, unheard kind
That is not in the world.

Chapter 13

"Sorry, I read the letter," Esmae said when she walked in on Myrtle making tea the next morning.

"Hmmmm," Myrtle said as she raised her eyebrows and looked at Esmae over her teacup as she took a sip. "Anything else?"

Esmae felt awkward as Myrtle continued to sip her tea and look at her.

"I'm sorry," Esmae said again.

"Oh, sweetie," Myrtle chuckled. "I knew you would." Myrtle put down her teacup and patted Esmae's arm. "What did it say?"

Excitement over the letter made Esmae chatty as she led Myrtle to the chairs and the fireplace. She couldn't wait to hand Myrtle the letter.

When Myrtle put it down, tears streamed down her cheeks. The love Paddy expressed, that Maeve had shared with him, reminded her of what she had with Earl, the lord and king of her heart.

Esmae handed her tissues. And they both blew their

noses and sounded like dueling honking geese.

"What do we do now?" Esmae asked and took a sip of tea, the warmth coating her insides. The heat from the cup warmed both of her hands as she put it on the table and held it there. "The book seems to be the next step. But the book could be anywhere."

Myrtle reached over and rested her hand on Esmae's arm. "Yes, it could." A comforting smile etched Myrtle's face. "But according to Evelyn, the book has to be in this shop."

Incredulity rushed through Esmae. "How…?"

Myrtle explained her last night's visit was with Michael one of Evelyn's nephews, and they called Evelyn in Florida.

"She said the book would have been donated with some other of her mother's things," Myrtle glanced around at the books. "Evelyn said her mother insisted, when the time came, that this shoppe by the only place they donate their things to."

"Did she say what it looked like?"

"No."

"Or if she wanted them back?"

"No, she doesn't," Myrtle squeezed Esmae's arm. "But that's a longer story, I promise to tell later."

"How…," Esmae asked again, turning to look over the piles of books and curiosities. "How are we going to find the book?"

"As they say," Myrtle's eyes twinkled with determination and humor, "War, but first coffee."

"Who?" Esmae laughed and shook her head. "Who says that?"

"My Earl," Myrtle smiled wistfully. "Whenever there was a daunting task ahead of us, he'd enjoyed the extra kick coffee gave him." Myrtle picked up her teacup. "We, of course, don't have to have coffee." And took a sip. Esmae picked up her teacup, too, and looked around.

The idea of how daunting this task was formed a pit in Esmae's stomach that couldn't be filled with the warmth of the tea or by Myrtle's optimism. Between the dark, creepy basement filled with odds and ends, to the shop area, to the attic, the idea of searching for a book they didn't know what it looked like, was overwhelming.

"But not impossible," Myrtle said as if she had read Esmae's mind. "And you, my dear, are connected to it, like you are the ink. The book is filled with it. When you get close…"

At that moment, Saturday morning's sun streamed through the windows situated above the bookshelves, making the shadows disappear into the corners. Esmae reached up and the sunlight brightened and warmed her hand.

"I won't be able to see any glow with this sun," Esmae

whispered. She didn't want to be contrary to Myrtle, but this task of finding the book was strewn with obstacles.

"Hmmmm….," Myrtle sipped her tea and contemplated this dilemma.

Esmae didn't interrupt and sipped her tea, looking at Myrtle, then at the rainbow colors the prisms twinkled on the walls, books, and pictures as the sun shone on them. Each one like a unique snowflake. Esmae concentrated on them and not on her worries and concerns.

The ink well began to glow gently, almost inconspicuously, on the mantle as the sunshine brightened and dampened the ink well's luminosity. This affirmed to Esmae how any connection to the ink well's glow would not help find the book on such a sunny day.

With a gentle nudge, Myrtle pointed to the faint glow. "Maybe we should trust that you'll find it," she said. "Trust that the book is meant for you."

"The ink well seems to glow stronger when I need it to," Esmae said in recognition. "But still…."

"Let go and let God, as they say," Myrtle raised her cup to Esmae. "Here's to the powers that be."

As they refreshed their tea from the teapot, they began a planning a course of action. If the book glowed like the ink well, then close to the ink well should make a connection if Esmae carried it around with her. With the sun streaming in, the glow would be faint and difficult to see.

"And what if…"

"Dear," Myrtle stopped her. "We're going to trust."

Within a few more minutes, Myrtle had gathered incense, sage, and two feather dusters. She lit the sage and waved it as she walked up and down the aisles. Esmae followed behind her.

"That's to cleanse anything that will interfere with any shadows and lack of faith," Myrtle put the sage down on its shell holder on the fireplace.

Next, she took three different kinds of incense.

"Lavender for peace," she lit the first one and stuck it in upright into a holder. "This next incense combines ginger masala, clove, and vanilla to invoke a connection with love." Myrtle stuck it in the holder next to the lavender. "And this sandalwood with a hint of wildflowers will give us good luck." After sticking it in the holder next to the other two incense, Myrtle lit them, let them burn for a bit, then blew the flame out allowing the smoke to waft into the air.

"And this?" Esmae held up the feather duster.

"Well," Myrtle laughed. "Might as well dust as we go. Since we've been meaning to." She grabbed the other feather duster.

"We might need some Pledge and a few rags."

Turning, Myrtle presented the rags and a can of

Pledge from behind her.

"Perfect," Esmae chuckled at how Myrtle thought of everything. She hugged Myrtle then grabbed a rag and a can on her way to the front of the store.

Myrtle called after Esmae.

"Take the ink well with you."

Chapter 14

Within the first five minutes, Esmae knew the feather duster wouldn't leave the kind of clean they needed. The feather dusters displaced the dust, casting them into the air to interfere with the sunlight and reflect its whiteness and the prism colors. Then it settled where it wanted, not as thick as before, but not removed either.

Instead Esmae opted to spray the rag with Pledge and completely remove the dust. On every bookshelf, she wiped the exteriors of the books as well as a shelf of knick-knacks. Within a few shelves, the rag was thick with dust and needed to be replaced. The glowing ink well moved with Esmae and shined dimly on the book bindings and titles. When dust was removed, the books' exteriors brighten, but no glow indicated it was the book Paddy had mentioned in his letter.

While Esmae had started at the front of the shop, Myrtle started behind the checkout counter where a stack of first editions and other rare books were kept.

As the sun moved across the sky, the twinkles of

prism moved, too. When customers came in, Myrtle assisted them while Esmae continued to dust shelves, books, oddities, and curiosities.

From nine in the morning to three in the afternoon, she meticulously dusted from the front to the back of the shop, only stopping for lunch and a spot of tea where Myrtle's words of encouragement kept her going.

"The book is here," Myrtle said. "I know it is. I feel it in my bones." After ten to twenty years, what it looked like or where it had been placed was buried deep in her memory. But her intuition and knowing it had been donated here by the family, meant the book was hidden on these shelves somewhere.

By four, Esmae lost motivation and energy. The fall sky began to set, immersing the back of the shop in shadows. This late in the afternoon, the ink well's bluish, soft fairy light surround only the space Esmae occupied. To her, the glow was like a candle and a welcome relief to the harsh fluorescent lights which flickered throughout the day. Except for today, mostly, they were never turned on. Strategically placed lamps lit the way.

Spray and wipe, moving up and down a singular bookshelf, visiting every book and nook and cranny. Trying to notice any unusual title or glow emanating from any sliver. Then move the ink well and the short four-step ladder to the next section. Spray, wipe, and repeat the process and continue the search.

With a stretch to remove the kinks and tightened muscles, Esmae stood on the top of the ladder and surveyed how much she had accomplished, then sighed with discouragement at the dark, back wall and sides she still had to do. Nothing stood out. Nothing glowed. The ink well hadn't been the beacon for the book they hoped it would be.

From behind her, a hand reached out to touch her back, a soft voice whispered her name. "Esmae…"

The touch sent a chill through Esmae and she lurched forward, startled, and almost fell off the short ladder. Esmae grabbed the edge of the bookshelf to steady herself. She turned, the aisle of bookshelves seemed long, narrow, and, past the glow of the ink well, dark until the end where a lamp glowed and, beyond that, the evening sun shined in a crimson diagonal line through windows Esmae couldn't see. No noise deepened the moment's solitude.

"Esmae?" Myrtle was right beside her. Her voice and touch startled Esmae further and made her catch the sides of the shelves, again, in her surprise. The bluish glow illuminated only Myrtle's pale face and enhance her blue-grey eyes, her body seemed to disappear, making her appear as a bobbing head.

"Oh, Myrtle," Esmae said, caught between a laugh and panic. "Was that you? I didn't see you." She shakily stepped down off the steps to the floor, touched Myrtle's shoulder, making sure it was her and not an apparition, . "I thought I felt someone, but when I looked, no one was there."

"Hmmmm," Myrtle looked concerned as she looked around. Then turned back to Esmae and smiled. "Just me, my dear." Myrtle took the ink well off the shelf and guided Esmae back to the corner, where a chair and table were barely visible until she placed the ink well on the table near a saucer with two cookie biscuits balanced on either side of a teacup. "You've done so much. Sit, relax," Myrtle said, patting Esmae's back.

"Oh, we've got company," Myrtle smiled. "Back in a jiffy." The cacophony of the bell's jingle and door's creak made Myrtle seem to quickly float down the bookshelf tunnel to the front of the store.

Grateful for the rest, Esmae relaxed deeper into the soft cushioned chair. Picking up the cup, she sipped the black English tea with sugar and milk, the exact recipe she liked, and surveyed and planned her next steps. About twenty more bookcases. At least ten behind her on the back wall, with seven up the wall on her right side and five up the wall after the door to the bathroom, on her left. About a minute per shelf, another minute to deep clean if a book needed it or there were extra knick-knacks on the shelf. Then another minute to dust the books at the top, all the while trying to pay attention to the titles to see if anything unusual stood out, which meant about five to ten minutes per bookshelf.

A nagging suspicion someone might have bought the book if it had been on these shelves for ten to twenty years, permeated Esmae's thoughts. Without the pen and ink, they wouldn't be able to write in it, which meant they might have thrown it away or donated it to another bookstore, school, or thrift store. Holding the teacup between her hands to warm them, Esmae closed her eyes. The book may be lost to her.

How badly do you want it? The Irish voice asked.

Esmae wasn't sure and didn't know how to answer. How badly *did* she want to find this book? Better yet, why. Was it out of curiosity or prying into someone's lifetime of love? *Maybe I wonder how anyone could find love and make it last passionately for over thirty or forty years.* Esmae knew she hadn't found love like that. The sad revelation made her heart ache. *Yet, I would stay for my children and grandchildren*, Esmae thought. *For all the memories and having a stable family. I would give up my happiness and the idea of romantic love for them. I would sacrifice for my family.*

Then this puzzle came into her life and the adventure of finding this book.

Maybe she could find the book, find a transcendental love, a true love, a forever love, the kind written about, and still try and make this life work. Maybe the book would help her cope with the lack of love from Sparky. She believed everyone deserved to find a once-upon-a-time, a once-in-a-lifetime kind of love. But what if that love wasn't the happily-ever-after kind in fairy tales and the love she was supposed to have was written in a book?

To find a book who loved me, written just for me, might be enough. I've always loved books. Esmae smiled at the thought. Books were her companions. Thinking about all the books she had read from an early age until now made her heart glow and her face radiate an internal bliss and universal recognition.

Every author of every book had an inspired motivate and reason to write. They might not realize a specific who they were writing for, but they were compelled, perhaps even driven, to write stories which would inspire, entertain, and touch people's lives. In a way, every book wanted the reader to feel the love and dedication it was written with—the essence behind the words—the time, energy, dedication, and sustained enthusiasm it took to create a book. With every word, an author wanted the reader to feel loved and to be inspired to share that love with others.

These insights and revelations grew as Esmae

appreciated each book she had read, each book she had touched and taken care of that day, and each book she was yet to know as she finished her task.

A radiant brightness from behind her encapsuled the dim glow of the ink well as it surrounded Esmae. Details of the shelves in front of her, which had been dim and unreadable before, were easily seen now. Esmae turned, blinded by its brightness. She closed her eyes, rubbed them, and slowly opened. As her eyes adjusted, the light seemed to cascade off the top of the bookshelf, pouring from the cracks between a couple stacks of books.

Esmae retrieved the step stool and, after moving the table and pushing the chair to the side, placed the stool in the now vacant location and as tight into the corner as possible. Stepping up the four steps, Esmae saw how books had been stacked and pressed into place, pushing whatever was making the cascading glow far back into the corner.

Two deep bookshelves came together, creating a deep corner. In a kitchen, this would be considered almost useless space, sometimes remedied by a lazy Susan. There were no lazy Susans on top of bookshelves in corners of bookstores, making it easy to add books to the top and lose others shoved far back into the corner. The abundant stack of books left only a few inches of space between the ceiling and books. If there hadn't been a few inches between the piles, the radiant glow would have been lost behind in the corner void, smothered by the stacks, and never seen again.

Esmae reached up and grabbed a few of the books from the stack, exposing more of the glow. With the books under one arm, and the other holding the shelf for balance, she carefully took a few steps backward down the step stool and put the books on the chair. Within seconds, Esmae walked back up and repeated removing the books exposing more of the glow, then stacking them haphazardly in the chair. Books on meditation, the otherworld, art, and others had blocked the book they had been searching for.

Finally, with twelve books of various sizes removed, Esmae stood on her tippy toes trying to see what was creating the glow. She was sure it was the book. It had to be the book, but it was still pushed too far back in the corner, so she couldn't see anything but the glow.

Her heart pounded as she tried to stand higher on her toes and reach for it. Esmae stood precariously on the tiptoes of one foot, bent her head, and reached up, pressing her right arm into the shelves for support. She stretched.

Electricity surged through her as her fingertips felt a book like no other. The outside was hard, cold metal, but smoothed with curves and dips.

Her fingernails scrapped across the outside making no sound as Esmae tried to use them to pull on one of the grooves, but her fingernails were too short and the book was too heavy. Unable to get a solid grasp, and her calf cramping, Esmae pulled her arm back and collapsed on the top step of the stool to massage her calf and slip off her shoe to knead the sole of her foot and pulled on her toes.

What to do. What to do. Esmae muddled and looked around for ideas. Grabbing one of the thicker books she had removed, she placed it on the top step of the stool. *A couple inches should help.*

Esmae stood on top of the book and jiggled back and forth. The book seemed stable and likely wouldn't slip off the stool. Determination made Esmae not think about it too much and, within a second, she was back on her tiptoes and leaning her left side into the bookshelf, stretching her hand and arm over the top to the glowing object in the corner.

Feeling along the front of the book Esmae came across a clasp. After fiddling with it for a few minutes, she closed her eyes, took a deep breath to calm her nerves and her pounding heart, and began slowly exploring the edges, following it to the top cover where it was hooked onto a....a latch? Esmae wondered. Flipping this small flap seemed easier than trying to move a heavy book with her fingertips.

She fiddled with the latch. Her fingertips trying to catch the corner, her eyes closed as Esmae tried to visualize flipping it without being able to see what she was doing. First try. She didn't have enough leverage. Esmae felt for the back edge of the latch. Second try. Something stopped the latch as she pushed up. Feeling on the inside of the latch, she found something stuck in a closed hook. One ended was pointed and the other had a thin metal chain attached. She pulled the chain and removed the pointed bolt. During the third try, her leg cramped and Esmae sat down again to massage her legs and give herself a break. Sweat dripped from her forehead and she breathed hard from exertion and excitement.

Tiptoeing on the book and arching her arm over the edge of the bookcase as far as she could stretch, the fourth try brought success. As soon as it was flipped, the metal latch became the closest piece of book to her.

Keeping her eyes closed, she was able to bend the latch completely toward her and grasp it between two fingers and her thumb. This allowed the book to be tugged, with each tug inching it toward her. After about five inches, Esmae was able to grasp the flap with all of her fingers and tug more fiercely. The book scrapped against the wooden top of the bookcase, and stopped.

Esmae tugged again and it wouldn't budge. She tried

tugging harder, but the book wouldn't move. Still not being able to see the book over the edge of the bookcase, Esmae felt along the edge of book to see what it might be caught on. With her fingers, Esmae felt a thick, round metal cylinder with a flat top. Esmae pushed the book back a half inch off the nail, then tried bending the nail over to the side. The nail dug into Esmae's fingertips as the thickness of the nail and the angle of her grasp made it impossible to bend.

Feeling along the edge of the book, Esmae wiggled her fingertips under the book, lifting it enough to fit most of her fingertips underneath the book's back cover. When she tried to lift it up, the book's weight strained Esmae's hand and she withdrew it to rub the pain from her wrist.

Not giving up, she reached back in, found the latch, leveraged the book, and pulled. She was hoping the bottom of the book wasn't as elaborately carved as the top and would slide over the nail with ease.

No such luck.

Esmae pulled the flap, and as the book slid on to the nail, it hooked on the ornamental grooves and got stuck.

Obstacles are there not to stop us, the Irish voice interjected, *but to show us how much we want something.*

Esmae hated platitudes, no matter how right that one was in this situation. A pain shot up her arm as it started to cramp from being in an awkward position for so long.

"Ugh," Esmae said as she pulled her arm back from the top of the bookshelf and shook it, relieving the cramp and tingling feel of pins and needles in her arm.

Frustrated, Esmae steadied herself by holding the bookcase as she stepped down off the book then off the stool. She took a few steps back and stared at the glow from the book she still couldn't see.

Tapping her foot as she stood with her hands on her hips, she looked up at her unseen goal. The light teased at what was beyond her sight to bring down.

Anger at her inability to retrieve this ancient, kismet book enhanced her frustration and her disappointment in herself. A lump formed in her throat and Esmae held back tears. Her thoughts raced, but none of them were a solution to the problem at hand. A lonely tear flowed down her cheek, and she quickly wiped it away. On a deeper level, disappointment was why she hated change or going after what she wanted. She just wanted life to be steady, predictable, stable. What the hell was she thinking wanting to find this book? What did she think it would change?

More tears fell and Esmae ignored them. Turning away from her source of frustration, she walked away, pacing to the end of the aisle and to the end of the next aisle, until she couldn't see the glow of the book. Each step she took, the book's light dimmed.

Finally far enough away to release her frustration and not think about the book, Esmae twisted her back, then stretched her arm back and forth and circled both of arms at the shoulders. Next, she cracked her neck by leaning it to the right, to the left, and forward toward her chest. Cupping her hands behind her head, she pressed her neck down into a deeper stretch, one she felt down her spine to the middle of her back. A few vertebrae cracked as tension was released.

She shook her arms and looked up. Her jaw tightened and her eyes narrowed with determination.

Even if this book didn't change her life, a nail, an obstacle she couldn't see, wasn't going to stop her. Not when she was this close. Her grandma always reminded her of a saying her mom had, "Curiosity killed the cat. Satisfaction brought him—or her—back." Esmae wasn't exactly sure what that meant, but she did have a curiosity to know what the book held for her. The ideas of being satisfied may not literally give her another life, but it revived her desire to see what the book might have inside.

"What to do…" Esmae looked around for ideas as she walked back to the corner, the book's light brightened as she got closer. Books were everywhere, Pledge, rags…no, that would snag on the nail also. The ink well glowed on the table, along with the saucer…that was smooth, but too small for her to fit under the book. Esmae stared at the books in the chair. All different sizes, along with a thin long one.

Esmae picked it up and considered its dimensions, about fourteen inches long seven inches wide, and a half inch thick. Most importantly, the front and back were smooth. *Almost a leather quality,* Esmae thought as she turned it over. "Travel Abroad" was embossed in gold lettering with smaller initials MFY embossed at the bottom. Opening it up, Esmae saw it was a travel journal. Each page had a place for the date, time, country, and details. None of the pages had been filled in. Whoever MFY had been, they had never traveled.

The understanding that many people did not travel far from their home made little impression on Esmae. The *Like me* thought accompanied acceptance of her world without a ting of sadness. That's how life was. But, this book could slip underneath the metal one, separate it from the nail, then slide it the rest of the way to her.

*To make this work as efficiently as possible...*Esmae's actions went faster than her thoughts as she gathered up three more of the thicker books and stacked them on the top step of the stool. Two books for each foot, about the same height...*Solidly stacked...*she didn't want to think any other way.

With the travel journal in hand, Esmae grasped the bookshelves to steady herself. Step, step, step, and a high step onto the books. First one foot. *That's solid. No wiggle.* Esmae took the last step and tried to sway the books and stool back and forth as she held onto the shelves. *Yep, good enough.*

Reaching up with the book in one hand and feeling with the second, Esmae stood on her tiptoes on top of the extra four or five inches. This made them less stable, but Esmae was beyond the precariousness of the situation and focused on being able to reach the book.

She pressed her face into the shelves and stretched up. Feeling the edge of the book, she lifted the one side with her free hand and shook it a bit to free it from the nail. When she could feel its freedom, she pushed the travel journal between the nail and the metal book, released the book, allowing it to rest on the nail head. Esmae pulled the journal and the metal book at the same time with both hands. With a few more seconds and multiple tugs, the metal object was in sight. Esmae lifted it down from the top of the bookcase, and realized it wasn't a book at all but a box.

With the heavy, metal box fully in her hands, the stool wobbled with their weight.

The lid of the box was loose, and the glow pierced through the cracks, shining upward and blinding Esmae as she clutched it to her chest as she stepped down and turned the box sideways, away from her face, to shine down the narrow aisle and illuminate the high walls of books.

The travel journal was left in the same place it had been found, unused and forgotten once again.

Chapter 15

"I found the book," Esmae said with such softness Myrtle wasn't sure she heard her correctly. With a thunk, Esmae put the metal box, which stored the kismet book inside, on the counter. She strained to be gentle, but it thudded and scratched the wood with its weight. The cover shone with iridescent luminosity as Esmae lightly touched the ornate embellishments of leaves, swirls, flowers, and unfamiliar symbols. The iridescence appeared in waves and brightened in spots where Esmae touched it.

The glow seeped from inside the metal box and through the cracks from where the lid warped as it met the thick middle. The middle of the metal box was carved on three sides to resemble pages in a book. The spine was carved with embellishments and symbols. No title was evident on any side. The metal latch fit snuggly over a metal semi-circle, which could be secured by a small metal thorn. This was attached to a metal chain which was welded to the top spine of the box.

With Myrtle by her side, Esmae unlatched the metal box and slowly flipped the lid open. The metal hinges remained silent, despite the dust and age. A substance, similar to the ink in the ink well, was coated on the inside of the lid and glowed continuously without waver.

A brown leather pouch lay inside, surrounded and protected by a dark velvet inlay. Esmae lifted the pouch out of its confinement. Tied leather strings secured the pouch, safely guarding the kismet book inside. The softness of the leather evoked a feeling of comfort in Esmae, and she held it out for Myrtle to feel.

Myrtle touched it and nodded her agreement. Putting the leather pouch down between them, Esmae struggled with the knots. At some point, water and heat had shrunk the leather, making it almost impossible to undo the knots.

"Here," Myrtle said, reaching under the counter and pulling out a sewing kit. She took a seam ripper and applied the sharp end to the knot. Even after five minutes and both of them tugging and trying, the knots did not loosen.

Pressing her lips together, Myrtle pulled out the small sewing scissors. They looked at each other. To cut something so old and revered seemed sacrilegious.

Without words, the conversation between them came to one question.

Do we have to?

There's no other way.

This was one of the oldest books either of them had the opportunity to touch and explore. Myrtle hesitated with the weight of their decision, then cut the string at the knot, allowing the leather pouch to open and reveal a hard leather book which also flowed with changing iridescent colors.

They stood, mesmerized by the kaleidoscope of color, mixing in random order, fading, swirling, almost dancing. Shades and designs of orange to red to yellow to green to blue to purple, all the colors, even those imperceptible to the naked eye, appeared. Colors, tones, and designs they never thought possible.

Esmae gently poked at it, her fingertip leaving a purplish mark on the cover. Lifting it out of the pouch with both hands and without letting go, Esmae's constant touch made the kaleidoscope slow and finally stop at a deep amethyst purple. Myrtle placed her hand over the cover and touched it with her fingertip, turning the spot a dark brown, almost black.

"The magic must only work for you," Myrtle said.

Esmae felt bad, she wanted Myrtle to share in this discovery and in its magic.

"No, no, dearest," Myrtle said, patting Esmae's arm. "I've had my great love. Earl and I were lucky to have decades together, like Paddy and Maeve. The universe is calling you. This kismet book is for you."

Tears welled up in Esmae's eyes as she realized she had rarely felt special and hadn't for decades. If life was to be explored, beyond the simplicity of her life, she wasn't sure she was ready. Change scared her. Maybe she didn't want this. Maybe this universal kismet had gotten it wrong.

She placed the book back on the leather pouch. Her heartbeat sped up and perspiration beaded on her forehead as she took a step back, staring at the book.

A warm hand on her forearm made Esmae look into Myrtle's kind, soft eyes.

"One step at a time," Myrtle said. "You don't know what will happen. Don't overthink this. You're going to be alright."

Was it the calm way in which Myrtle spoke or the warmth traveling up her arm and through her body that made Esmae's heart slowdown and the tight grip of panic dissipate, Esmae wasn't sure. Change and adventure were not her fortes. In her whole life, she hadn't traveled more than six hours from where she was born, and she stayed married because, well, there was a comfort in the known. If the book was calling her to be someone she wasn't, Esmae couldn't do that.

Myrtle's words interrupted her thoughts. "You'll

never be given more than you can handle," Myrtle squeezed Esmae's arm. "And you've already handled a lot. You can handle this, too, it's a book. Sure, a book with a touch of magic. And, one that's meant for you."

As if on cue, the book rippled shades of purple and blue from the center of its cover, like a pebble being thrown into a lake at sunset.

There's keen delight in what we have, the Irish voice, which seemed louder and more distinct than ever before, added to calm Esmae as she watched the book. *The rattle of pebbles on the shore, under the receding wave.*

There was a pause as the ripples grew thicker and reverberated with some sky pinks and sea greens among the purples and blues of the water. Esmae whispered the words as they were spoken.

I hear lake water lapping with low sounds by the shore;
While I stand on the roadway, or on the pavements gray,
I hear it in the deep heart's core.

Esmae thought she could hear the lake waves and the ripples hitting the shore. His voice gave Esmae the courage to take a step toward the book with appreciative wonder.

She caressed the book, feeling the softness of the leather, the engraved designs, similar to those on outer metal book. The ripples didn't stop when Esmae picked it up, but vibrated subtly, sending an electrical charge through her. Her heart, which had beat rapidly out of panic, now gave her an ethereal sense she had come home.

Her cheeks reddened as her face shined from the inside out.

"Go sit down, my dear," Myrtle said, not touching her as she noticed the physical changes Esmae was going through. "I'll make a new pot of tea. I think this calls for some Harney and Sons cinnamon sunset."

Esmae hugged the book close to her chest, feeling herself silently absorb its presence and commune with it silently, like it was a long, lost friend. She didn't verbally understand what was being said, but internally she felt an intuitive and sublime difference which evoked a feeling of awe. She didn't want this. She didn't want change. But she was drawn to it, like a moth to a flame.

The fire warmed her and the book as they sat in the chair, Esmae slowly rocking the book like it was a part of her. The rhythm of the book changed from ripples created by pebbles to the pulse and quiver of a flame. The underlying color of the book was still purple intermingled with flickering shades of gold, orange, and dark red.

The edges of the pages were ragged, brown, and rough from use and age. Esmae felt these with her fingertips, learning the feel and details of her new friend.

When the time felt right, she placed the book on her

lap and carefully opened the cover. The pages within were white and crisp, contrasting sharply with the edges. Esmae brushed her fingers across the page feeling its smoothness as she turned the first page and a few more. No writing or marks were on these first pages.

On the upper two-thirds of the sixth and seventh pages, a sketch of ocean waves covered both. The sun low in the background, a reflection in the water, rocks along the side, and three squiggles in the air representing birds. Printed underneath the waves: "The world is full of magic things, patiently waiting for our senses to grow sharper." Then in script, in a corner were the words, "I will wait, patiently."

Esmae studied the details of the ink-sketched picture, noticing the individual waves, the sun reflected in the water, and the broken pieces of rock and shells scattered across the beach. On the left, reeds almost hid an island nestled faraway in the background, sitting on the horizon with the setting sun.

Esmae turned the next few blank pages to the written words she had heard in her head. She shuffled through the pages to the last page written on. There they were, the words she had heard the Irish voice say in her head earlier that day.

There's keen delight in what we have,
The rattle of pebbles on the shore, under the receding wave.

There was blank space between those lines and the next.

I hear lake water lapping with low sounds by the shore;
While I stand on the roadway, or on the pavements gray,
I hear it in the deep heart's core.

Esmae's head spun as she tried to comprehend that her inner Irish voice spoke the words written in this book.

She turned to the first pages which she assumed must have been written years ago, when she first heard the Irish voice. Handwritten words followed by a substantial paragraph or two of space. These spaces seemed interjected, like what was written wasn't complete. Like he was going to come back and add to what he had written. Or, maybe, he was waiting for someone to respond.

At the top the page, a quote was offset with bold words -- letters written over and over again to make them bold. Esmae whispered them.

"In all the world, there is no heart for me like yours. In all the world, there is no love for you like mine."

Maybe the Irish voice wasn't a voice, but this book calling to her, loving her, knowing her.

"The book who loved me," Esmae flipped through the pages, scanning the words. Some so intimate and private she was embarrassed to see them written down.

Thinking there was someone through this book reaching out to her was too surreal to think about and trying to understand it made Esmae's head hurt. She would focus on the tangible, on what was right in front of her, the rest would figure itself out.

Esmae contemplated how she should respond to this intimacy, these words written especially for her.

After taking the ink well and pen down from the fireplace, Esmae found the first pages with the ocean waves and the sunset. Dipping the pen in the glowing ink and then sliding the pen tip across the top of the bottle to remove the excess ink, Esmae's hand shook slightly as she put pen to paper under the quote already there. Carefully and slowly she wrote in cursive, making sure each letter was defined and flowed together with the next. The ink glowed until it dried on the paper, like sending it off to parts unknown: Words are the only true magic.

Words are the only true magic.

Chapter 16

Who mocks at music mocks at love, the Irish voice said. And Esmae wondered if these words, too, were being written in the book at the moment she heard them. Her heart raced at the thought.

"These pissants," Sparky laughed into Esmae's ear so no one else could hear. "Trying to be a Beach Boys cover band."

The Irish words, "who mocks at music mocks at love" made Esmae look at Sparky as a tapestry with cigarette burns and frayed edges. She swallowed what she wanted to say, instead she smiled at him and nodded her head in agreement. With their son with them, this wasn't the place nor time.

They entered through the double doors of the Pavilion as a family, grabbed a few snacks, and sat at a bar-height table by an open side door for fresh air and not too far from the front door. Sparky liked being early to get the best place to see everyone as they came in. He was warm, charming, and interesting to everyone.

"Dad," Albert said when the song ended. "There's some friends over there." Albert waved to a group of three boys standing outside the open side doors. "Mind if I..."

Sparky took a long drink of his beer, keeping his eyes on Albert's as he tipped the bottle upward to finish it. Then he slammed it on the table, making both Esmae and Albert jump. They didn't know what to expect as Sparky glared at his boy.

With a laugh, he put Albert's neck into a hold and rubbed his head. "Oh, my boy," Sparky chuckled. "Here." He pulled out twenty dollars. "Go buy your old man another brewski and keep the rest."

"But...," Albert hesitated. He looked down at the money then quickly at his mom and back to his dad. "What if they won't sell to me?"

"Bah," Sparky said. "Tell Cliff you're my son. You'll be fine."

Esmae wanted to say something, but Albert ran off to do his dad's bidding. They watched as Albert stood in line for a few minutes, then ordered at the bar. They saw Albert point in his parents' direction. Cliff looked over. Sparky waved, and Cliff nodded his head in response.

Soon Albert was walking over with two beers.

"Is that other for your mom?" Sparky asked, eyebrows raised innocently.

"Ah, sure…" Albert handed one beer to Sparky and put the other on the table in front of Esmae. He smiled weakly at his mom.

Sparky looked at the boys waiting for Albert, then back at Albert. The beer for Esmae sat on the table in front of her. She didn't like beer. Sparky took it and winked at her.

"Hide it in your front jean pocket," Sparky handed the beer to Albert, who stuck it in the pocket of his loose pants. "Now put your shirt over. If it feels unstable, stick your hands inside to hold it."

"Sparky," Esmae's concerned voice did nothing to stop him. He glared her into silence.

Albert incredulous look made Sparky laugh. "I used to be your age, too." He gave Albert an 'atta boy' pat on his shoulder. "Don't let them catch you…"

"Okay, thanks, Dad," Albert said as he hurried off.

"And don't get too drunk," Sparky said.

"Sparky…" Esmae said.

He turned abruptly to her. "He's sixteen almost seventeen. Drinking age is nineteen. He's got to learn how to hold his liquor now." Sparky shrugged his shoulders, turning his attention to the front door. "Besides, what teen doesn't drink."

That was it. The discussion was over. Esmae's concerns would not be listened to now nor had they with their other children.

"Look," Sparky took a swig of his beer. "There's Mylie and Vern." He waved them over to join them.

Within an hour, three tables had been pushed together. Within a few hours, five askew tables formed a contorted line. The beer bottles and wine glasses liberally decorating them, like ornaments on a flat, misshapen Christmas tree. The women at one end, the men at the other, fluctuating numbers of five to seven to ten couples as they danced, stepped outside, or moved around visiting other tables of friends.

From one end of the tables, Esmae looked at Sparky laughing and drinking at the other end. From the looks of it, he was on his tenth beer. Sparky looked at her, raised his chin slightly in acknowledgement, then continued the conversation with the group of guys around him.

She knew he was keeping an eye on her. There was power in being a couple in a town like this.

"So nice to see you out, Izzy," Lori said as she joined the group again after dancing with Brian.

"Nice to see you, too," Esmae wasn't sure if either of them cared, but that's how the pleasantries started. "How's little Matty?"

"Oh," Val beamed with pride. "Not so little anymore, yah know. He's attending NDSU..."

Esmae nodded as Val continued, then the rest of the

wives and mothers joined in, sharing the best of their children, pulling out pictures, taking pride in what they had created.

They chatted about jobs, church, upcoming holidays, and school fundraisers.

"Hey, sista," Jaci exuberance interrupted Esmae's thoughts and absentminded nodding to the conversations going on around her. "Long time no see. How've you been?" They hugged and laughed. Then took a step back to look at each other.

The twinkle of mischief and love of life oozed from Jaci's tattooed arms and black biker leather jacket. "You haven't changed a bit," Esmae laughed at her bestie from high school.

"Well, hun, you look like you need this." Jaci put one arm around Esmae's shoulder and handed her a leather-covered, tin flask with the other.

Shaking her head, Esmae refused. She looked down at the other end of the table where Jaci's husband, Dave, was chatting with Sparky. Probably keeping him busy so Jaci and her could talk.

"Just one," Jaci said. "We know you need one. Hell, deserve it."

The rest of the women looked away quickly and started chatting loudly with each other when Esmae looked around the table.

Embarrassment made tears well in Esmae's eyes and her heartbeat faster as she realized they probably knew about Sparky and had been observing her all night. That's what happened in small towns, and Sparky hadn't kept his philandering discreet.

This wasn't the kind of attention she could handle being the center of. She wasn't Sparky, who seemed to thrive and be in his element at the opposite end of the table chatting with the guys.

Though Jaci and Esmae had been besties in high school, life's circumstances tore them apart, rarely allowing them to spend time together. That was mostly Esmae's fault. She didn't want to face anyone the way she was. She still didn't. Esmae looked around, wanting to escape, forgetting Jaci was beside her.

"Take it," Jaci turned Esmae to her. Then, took the flask, unscrewed the top, and handed it to Esmae. "Drink."

The other women at the table joined in as a low rumble. "Drink, drink, drink…"

Esmae lifted the flask, threw back her head, and drank a long guzzle. Jägermeister, a cold, black licorice taste coated her mouth and burned her throat.

Esmae coughed when she finished, and Jaci hit her on her back.

"Well, that'll put hair on yer chest." She took the flask

and drank a long shot, then started passing it around.

"I need to give you some of my peach brandy," Esmae's eyes twinkled at Jaci. "Much smoother than that Jäger." She grabbed Jaci around the shoulders and laughed and coughed at the same time.

"But Jäger has always been our drink of choice," Jaci said. Back in high school and ever since, the few times they got together, they shared a shot of Jäger. Almost a tradition at this point.

"I would love to buy some," Lisa said. "I remember buying some at the school fundraiser a few years back. That was the best stuff."

"And your fruit wines," said another.

"Have you tried her roasted sugar pecans?"

The panic Esmae felt before was quelled by the Jäger and the compliments she was receiving about her liquor and baked goods. They didn't know how cheap Sparky was when it came to Christmas presents or donations to the bake sales, whether at school or church. Esmae needed to become creative during their first year of marriage, a particularly tough year financially for them. A local farmer, Arthur Carter, gave her a bunch of raspberries, strawberries, and blueberries from his garden. With twelve children, she wondered why he had given her so much. He said it was because his wife, Lillius, didn't like fruit or veggies, and he usually sold what he could. The batch he gave her was overripe and couldn't be eaten. But he had heard Esmae knew how to make fruit wine and jam. The amount of produce Arthur had given her, honed her jam and fruit wine skills. She gave some back to him and his family at Thanksgiving as a thank you.

The next year, Sparky took four bushels of peaches as payment for some work. She made jars and jars of peach brandy and jam. Some they sold, others they gave away as presents, and, at Christmas, she traded some for presents for the kids.

As the ladies raved about her wine, brandy, and jams, Esmae beamed with a sense of pride she never felt before and never knew was possible.

"I'll stop by sometime," Jaci said.

Esmae swallowed hard. Except for a few items to make small batches, all the equipment and everything she made was still at the house, at Sparky's house, in the basement.

"Iz," Jaci searched Esmae's face and put her arm around Esmae's shoulders again in a tight squeeze. "Have another," she said and handed Esmae the flask.

Sparky waved a few more couples over when the band took a break. Esmae recognized either both or one person of the couple as they gathered around the tables as classmates or from the neighboring Catholic school. Not all of the same class, but within a few years of each other. That's what made small towns special. Everyone knew everyone, including extended family. They cared, in some way or another, especially remembering the exploits and fun they had in their youth. This wasn't gossip, but shared memories and the gathering of stories.

At the head of the table, Sparky drew the attention of everyone by raising his beer and smashing it down on the table, and drinking it fast as it foamed over.

"Coach!" The men at the end yelled, raising their beer, wine, or liquor and taking a drink.

Esmae shook her head as she raised her glass of red wine with melted ice cubes. Sparky coached little league for a number of years as the kids grew up, and, even though he stopped about five years ago when Albert turned eleven, the guys still called him "Coach."

"Guess who…." Sparky stopped to build attention. Everyone at the tables quieted down, a few snickers and jittery laughs echoed from those who had played this drinking game before.

"Guess who…," Sparky looked around, studying each face. "Who among us…" he hesitated again, drawing out the tension. "Snatched the centerfold out of his dad's Playboy magazine and took it for show and tell in second grade? If you…"

A number of names were called out.

"Alright, if you get it wrong, you have to drink," Sparky said. "And it was…"

"Charlie!" A female voice yelled. "Husband loves telling that story and how furious his dad was about it."

"Thanks, baby," Charlie lifted his glass to his wife. "Always loved the female form. He he he."

Most people knew it was Charlie, but drank anyway.

"Was that in Mrs. Cook's class?"

"I bets she wasn't impressed…" A few more chattered and laughed at the details.

Now it was Charlie's turn. "Who…," he hesitated for effect, "pulled their pants down and mooned about a half dozen school buses while standing on the front steps of the school?"

Names were yelled out, like making stock market trades. Charlie pointed his beer across the table to Andrew. "To your hairy ass, my friend," he raised his beer and drank. "A sight I'll never forget."

Christi, Andrew's wife, smacked his butt, then shouted. "Hasn't changed in thirty some years." Beer spurted from a few as they couldn't contain their laughter.

Andrew whispered teasingly in his wife's ear, "And you love my hairy ass, you wench."

She pulled back and looked into his eyes. "I do, every last hair." Then kissed him with passionate innuendo of what might happen later that night, if they didn't get too drunk.

Gary bumped into Andrew, but Andrew waved him off. "I'm taking this one," Gary said. No one cared, they just liked to relive the stories and memories of yesteryear. "Who…," Gary started with the obligatory pause. "Sold Marlboro cigarette coupons to kids telling them they were circus tickets in first grade. Now, he's a law enforcement officer."

Laughter and raised beers to Bill, who bowed and raised his beer in surrender.

Bill continued, "In his senior year, he wrote his own excuses every Wednesday during ski season for ditching school."

People looked around trying to decide who might have done it as Sparky and Bill laughed. "Bill," Sparky yelled. "That was Bill again."

"Oh, Bill," many said as they drank.

Others started to share.

"Turned 19 in high school. Had a fake ID. Went down to the bar at lunch to have a hamburger and beer with his friends. They all came back drunk."

"Asked out the Spanish teacher about hundred times during his junior and senior year."

"She was hot."

"I told my French teacher to get her hairy armpits out

of my face. I got chucked out of class."

"Teachers were having a celebration and I spiked their punch with pure alcohol."

"When was this?"

"Did you get caught?"

"Nah, but I'm still ashamed of it thirty years later. I think a few of the teachers were recovering alcoholics."

"Here's to Trav Olson."

"Best math teacher and coach ever."

"Miss those pick-up games with him."

"The only teacher who insisted that we call him by his first name."

"Here, here."

Everyone raised their glass to Trav and reflected silently for a moment.

Then Bill broke the silence.

"Called Mr. Goowski 'goochie, goochie, gew'."

"We all did, just not to his face."

"Holding hands with the guy that I've been married to for 51 years," Mary Lou raised her beer and kissed her husband. "You can see how well that worked out."

"Whistling in seventh grade. I still can't whistle and I got into trouble."

"Farting during morning prayers in front of a nun."

"Turned the clocks back fifteen minutes as a senior prank."

"Remember when Norma went into the boy's locker room to confront a guy who she had gone out with. He told everyone he had his way with her and she wasn't having it. So she got into his face and made him confess to everyone there that he had made the whole thing up."

"That took some balls," Jaci said, raising her flask to Norma.

Norma raised her beer back, "Yep, got called into the principal's office for that. But when he heard the story, I didn't get suspended, only a stern warning not to do it again."

"Who was the guy?" Someone asked.

Norma smiled a crooked smile and shook her head. "Some details shouldn't be relived." And she took a long swallow.

"Who…" Ronald's drunken voice loudly interrupted the individual conversations to draw attention. "Who…took Polaroids of his naked, sleeping girlfriend and show-ed them to everyone? And when he lost one and someone found it, he got into a fight…" A loud belch ended the sentence.

Whispers and conversations were drown out as the band began playing. The game over, individual conversations began, and a few couples finished their drinks and headed to the dance floor.

Esmae saw Sparky put his arm around Ronald and

lead him outside.

Esmae listened to the conversations around her without participating. Weariness from the long day started to make her sleepy. She looked up, and saw Albert tap his father on the shoulder. Sparky leaned over to have Albert whisper in his ear, then smiled. He turned and patted Albert on the back again with an 'atta boy' pride. Sparky pulled out another twenty and gave it to Albert, who was gone within seconds after Esmae saw him mouth the words, "Thank you, Dad."

Sparky lifted his beer and looked down at Esmae, giving her a broad, arrogant, toothy smile, what some might call a shit-eating grin, daring her to say anything.

"Well," a man's voice whispered in her ear. "He's a wonderful father."

She knew that voice. Turning, she gave him a half-hug. "Kevin," she said. "Where have you been?"

They stepped away from the table to talk privately.

"Around," Kevin said. "Working. With it being so dry, there's been more fires."

"Have you talked to Myrtle?"

"Nope, haven't had the chance."

"We found something," Esmae grabbed his arm and looked earnestly into his eyes. "You need to come to the shop tomorrow. What we found...is really something extraordinary…"

"Hey, Kevin," the voice was cold as a hand pulled Esmae to him.

"Hey," Kevin's voice was equally as cold. "James."

Sparky hated to be called by his first name.

"So, you two have a date tomorrow?" Sparky asked.

"No," Esmae's brows furrowed together at Sparky. "That's not…"

"Myrtle needs some assistance," Kevin said. "We know you won't help."

"Maybe you should have paid more attention to your own wife."

The tension between them tightened and pulsed with a life of its own.

"Hey, everyone," Shawnda smiled brightly as she joined them, standing close to Kevin, not noticing the tightened stances of the men. "How's everything? Did you see there's going to be fireworks over the lake at midnight?"

Shawnda's exuberant entrance cut the tension and dissolved it to mere slivers.

"No, I hadn't seen that," Esmae hugged Shawnda. "So nice to see you." They smiled at each other. The two men looked around, ignoring each other.

"Want to watch them with me?" Shawnda pulled Kevin's arm drawing his attention to her.

He looked at her, trying to register what she said. "Um…"

Shawnda's face turned red from embarrassment, then drained white. "Sorry," she said. "I thought…"

"No, no…," Kevin looked from Shawnda to Esmae and Sparky and back again. "I would…sure." His gentle smile made Shawnda glow as her cheeks flushed and color came back into her face.

"Want to lead the way?" Kevin flourished his hand in the direction of the lake.

"Would love to," Shawnda's eyes widened and twinkled as she looked up at Kevin. She grabbed his outstretched hand as she started to walk away.

Sparky reached out and held Kevin's arm, stopping him from moving for a moment.

"Leave my wife alone," he growled, his voice low and full of threat.

Kevin pulled his arm out of Sparky's grasp. "It's not like that." He leaned into Sparky. "You don't appreciate what you have," and shook his head in disgust.

Esmae pulled Sparky back as Shawnda turned and pulled Kevin's hand to follow her.

"Let's get you a beer," Esmae said.

Sparky grabbed her by her shoulders and shook her, with short rapidity, then, realizing others at the table were looking, he embraced her, holding her close.

"If you ever sleep with him," Sparky whispered in her ear. "I'll kill you both." He pulled back and kissed her, leaning her into a dip and what others would see as a romantic gesture.

When he held her upright and released her, Esmae stumbled, unsteady from the threat and the kiss. She knew what it looked like to everyone else. Looks could be deceiving. That's what Sparky was good at.

Chapter 17

After the kiss, Esmae said goodbye, hugged her son and made sure he was sober, then left. With a smug, contented Cheshire cat smile on his face, Sparky hadn't tried to stop her.

She walked along Detroit Lake, the moon shining and reflecting on the water, waves lapping on the shore. In this peaceful moment, the Irish voice joined her.

I will arise and go now,
For always night and day
I hear lake water lapping
With low sounds by the shore;
While I stand on the roadway
Or on the pavements grey,
I hear it in the deep heart's core.

At midnight, she quietly unlocked Myrtle's shop and gathered the book, ink, and quill on the table in front of the fireplace. As Esmae turned the pages, the dried ink glowed faintly in the darkness of the shop.

Slowly, Esmae turned each page. There were sketches

here and there, but they were indistinguishable in the shadows of the night. To see better, she lit a candle, not wanting to turn on any lights to alarm Myrtle. Bringing it closer to the book, the words and images became clear. There was a fish, a thistle, rocks, a boat, detailed flames above a wood fire, a few doodles, and a piece of a story written in scrawling cursive.

Who mocks at music mocks at love, started the last page and was followed by words and details the Irish voice hadn't spoken.

"Who mocks at music mocks at love," Bill O'Brien spoke these words to his nephew.

"Twasn't me who said it," he told his nephew, Tieg. "Twas Yeats, who spoke to the good people on numerous occasions. If ye arn't careful, you'll have them to deal with."

Tieg was having none of it. Believing in fairies was for the older folks, the ones riddled with wild imaginings and lessons they wanted to teach the young.

"Oi'll have none of it," Tieg told his uncle. "The Devil take ye."

The color drained from Bill's face. He made three signs of the cross, knocked on the table three times, and grabbed his nephew by the front of his shirt.

"Take it back," he pulled his nephew closer and

looked earnestly in his eyes. Then softly whispered with great anguish. "Take it back, dear nephew. Take the curse back."

Tieg wanted to laugh, but the sincere panic in his uncle—whom he loved most in the family—stopped him. Tieg placed his hand on his uncle's, and looked sincerely into his eyes.

"Oi'll take it back," he said, then something took hold of him. Something hard he couldn't explain. "I'll take it back when they prove to me it *needs* taken back."

Then he knocked three times on the wooden table in mockery. "May the good people grant you any wish you want as a sign when they prove me wrong."

Bill tightened his hold on his nephew's shirt and then hugged him to his chest. Tieg rolled his eyes and allowed himself to be crushed for a few seconds, then tried pushing away. But Bill held on for dear life.

"Oh, nephew," Bill lamented. "What have ye done?"

Tieg finally pushed Bill away and scoffed. "Love ya, Unk, but nothin' is gonna hurt you." He handed a pint to Bill. Taking the other, he said, "Here's to the 'good people' and fairies of old. Slainte."

With nothing left to do, Bill drank along with his nephew.

Amidst their drinking, the strangest thing happened.

The entry ended there. And it shocked Esmae. This had nothing to do with what had happened to her, well, except there had been drinking. When she thought about the Irish voice and the words she had heard in her head, she thought it was connected to her everyday life in some way. Then, after reading how the book brought Paddy and Maeve together, she thought these entries would be like love letters to her.

This certainly wasn't a love letter to her. This was a story, an Irish story about the good people, which seemed to be a reference to fairies.

The person who wrote these entries must have no idea she could read them, must have no idea she existed.

Esmae felt the embossed symbols on the book, feeling its electricity as she puzzled at what the book held for her.

The book was a conduit connecting her to this mystery person who wrote these words on its pages. Written words he had no idea would make a difference in her life. Somehow the book allowed and filtered the words she needed to hear into her consciousness.

Esmae picked up the book, shuffled through its pages, and held it close. The book's energy pulsed like a heartbeat against her chest and synchronized with her own.

This wasn't the love story she expected. Maybe it was

because she was still married. Maybe this book wasn't her true love or, at least, not an ordinary love letter like what Paddy and Maeve had found, but a steppingstone to finding herself, to loving herself.

This wasn't a white knight riding in to rescue her, not that she ever expected something like that. But, whatever this was, it was a step away from what she had always accepted, a step away from the familiar and toward something unknown.

Scary as it was, Esmae knew if she kept doing what she had always done, she would always be what she had always been. A doormat for Sparky.

Taking a step toward the unknown, toward something different was the universe giving her not what she thought she wanted but what she needed.

Thoughts swirled in Esmae's head as she reasoned about the book and its purpose for her life.

This didn't seem like a step toward love. *Maybe this book was meant to give each recipient their unspoken desire.* Esmae thought. *Paddy and Maeve needed love. I need....* Esmae took brutal, heartfelt stock of what she truly needed. Her conclusion surprised her.

I need...to take a courageous step into the unknown. Esmae smiled contently at herself. *I can do that. I can do just one step.* Without the expectation she would love the person on the other side, she could—and would—do this for herself.

Looking down on an unfinished story, tiredness left her. Esmae dipped the quill into the ink. The glow illuminated her face and brightened the last words on the page. That's where she began to write.

Bill believed his nephew hadn't taken away the curse and his nephew believed neither had anything to fear. Esmae had read enough Yeats to know fairies should not be scorned.

Let the adventure begin.

Esmae continued to write into the wee hours of the morning. Ink stained her fingers with glowing specks.

Across the ocean on an Irish shore by the Aran Islands, a man watched in astonishment as words appeared, a bright glow which then faded on to the page letter by letter, word by word, sentences into paragraphs, adding to his story. The good people of fairies and selkies were finally answering the wish he made years ago when he first found the book.

This is not…

The End

ACKNOWLEDGEMENTS

Thank you to my editor, John Sutton, for his belief in my story from its earliest conceptual stages, for proofreading and editing, talking through arcs, contemplating ideas, developing characters — especially Simon, and for telling me about *tabula rasa* — the mind being in a blank or empty state. This fundamental idea, along with spirit and soul, influences the books and the characters' abilities to connect and communicate.

Thank you to the support and encouragement of my friends and family, especially my mom — Carol Sue, my dad — Ken, and my kids — Dain and Shalee. You are the best! This series will be better because of your belief and enthusiasm for me and this tale of romance.

Thank you to William Butler Yeats (1865-1939), a notable Irish poet, dramatist, prose writer, and a believer in Irish lore, myths, and legends. His words weave Esmae and Simon together. They aren't just characters but people whose stories we are trying to tell.

Thank you also to Pixabay artists and Canva for resources to make the cover and as an inspiration for other graphics.

Special acknowledgement to:
Jaci, Theresa, Cheryl, Shawn, Jennifer, Susan, Rachel, Lauri, Mylie, Amy, Tami, Velvet, Katie, Malissa, Mariann, Thomas, Sean, Nye Beach Book House, and so many others.

Thank you for your encouragement, prayers, and excitement for this series. I am truly grateful and humbly appreciative.

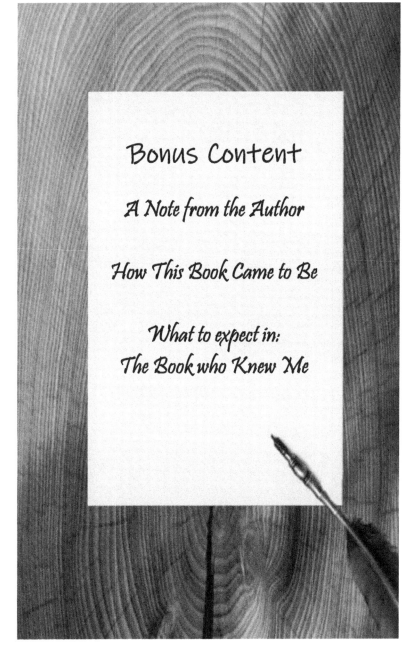

Bonus Content

A Note from the Author

How This Book Came to Be

What to expect in:
The Book who Knew Me

A Note from the Author

Dear Reader,

This is based on actual characters and ideas, as all stories are.

Every character is made up of bits and pieces of people I know. Yet, this book is fictious and all characters develop as a writer gets to know them and shares their story.

Esmae's personality and character quirks are based on my mom, grandma, and myself, while blended with her own unique attributes.

The husband of Esmae is based on my stepfather (who I saw choke my mother while saying "Why are you making me do this?"), a few guys I dated, and a few other men friends and family have either dated or been married to. Writing these scenes, especially those which happened in real life, made me cry. They were emotionally exhausting to write and edit. I found I needed to take breaks between scenes before I could continue telling the story these characters want me to tell.

These pieces make this story as true and as real as the

magic of any books we love and seem to love us in return in ways we feel and can't put into words.

Thinking about it, this story isn't just a story to me. Esmae may have some of the characteristics of people I know, including myself, but she is her own person. Some of the scenes I envisioned going one way, but they went another because of Esmae. I had to let her go through her own process and let her tell her story.

For example, I thought Esmae would find the pen, ink well, and book within the first few chapters. Took much longer then what I thought it would. The mystery, intrigue, and journey Esmae needed to go on developed as she came to life – or as I got to know her and the other characters in the story.

And, yes, Detroit Lakes is a real place. One of my most favorite places and one I spent much time in growing up. There is no bookstore like Myrtle's Book Shoppe in D.L., but other aspects are true, especially circa 1982.

The bookstore that I used as a guide is located in Newport, Oregon, and is called the Nye Beach Book House. I could spend hours there, and have. This, too, is one of my most favorite places, as is the Old Historic Bayfront on Bay Boulevard in Newport.

There is something charming, familiar, and special about Detroit Lakes — which is surrounded by Minnesota lakes and is where most of my friends and family live, and

Newport—on the central coast of Oregon, surrounded by the Pacific Ocean, and is where my son and I went deep sea fishing, crabbing, and where we vacationed with friends and family. My daughter was born in Oregon. I feel spiritually connected and pulled to both places.

The journey of writing this story is a personal one. As Esmae connects with who she is and what she wants in life, as well as how she will change, I feel like I am, too. I'm on this journey with her. I hope you feel the same way and wonder, as I do, exactly what will happen to her and with Simon.

The adventure is just beginning as the magic of life, love, and lore has much more to reveal.

Please, find me on Instagram @Sanz_Edwards. This is my author page. I will add more announcements, excerpts, and tidbits in the future.

Much love,

Sanz

How This Book Came to Be

In 2014, in a Facebook writing group, a person posted a prompt that went something like this: *Someone should write a book about the book falling in love with the reader.* Have to admit, my heart skipped a beat at the thought. As an avid reader, especially growing up on a farm without internet, only three tv channels, and my closest friend miles away with no vehicle, books were my constant companions. I loved books and their adventures, heroines and heroes, learning about faraway places and times, and the rocky road to finding true love.

Books are treasures to me. I can't walk into a bookstore without buying at least one. (Okay, someone might call this an addiction, but a healthy one. ;) haha) The older, the more worn, with that old book smell, the better, the more it tugs at my heart to buy it, to give it a good home, to treasure it. When I move, what I own most of—are books (and art supplies). My dream is to own a library like the one Belle receives from the Beast.

Readers fall in love with books inexplicitly. My daughter has reread her favorites, including three to four books in a series, at least 20 times, always finding something new.

This FB post prompted me to write about 20,000 words in the month of November 2015 for NaNoWriMo (National November Writing Month—to find out more, explore their website). To win NaNo, a person must write 50,000 words. I've never won NaNo.

The first 20,000 was all I could write for years. I tried writing more, but it didn't come together. Over the last six years, bits and pieces filled in the missing ideas, information, character development, and their arcs.

One hurdle I needed to get over was what I thought everyone else might think "a book who loved" would be like. This was my story to write, but is my characters' story to tell. Someone else will write and tell their characters' story in their unique way. (Note: If you have an idea about having a book fall in love with its reader, then you should write it. I know it will be uniquely yours and different than mine. Enjoy the journey with my best wishes for fun and success.)

Characters drive the action. Getting to know them and showing them to you, the reader, is a process of discovery and amazement for the writer. Characters take on a life of their own and their development creates the story.

From six years ago to the beginning of writing this story months ago, I didn't realize Yeats would play such an intricate role in connecting these two, Esmae and Simon. But, he does. There's magic in writing. As an author, it is like seeing these lives in a different dimension, and allowing words to connect the reader to this other world and the possibility of what is happening.

As I write, I find a transcendent truth to their trials, hopes, and the journey of discovery they need to go on to become the people they are destined to be. If you enjoyed the story, you related to and were encouraged by the characters and the journey they are going through.

Because, life isn't an easy journey. When I was young, living on that farm reading books, I thought life was much easier. I wanted to be a writer since I was 10 years-old. At that time, I possessed a naivete about the trials of life. I thought everything turned out, that good conquered all. Most of the time, every trial has a silver lining, but only when we decide good will come out of evil. Good is a choice, not a consequence. Took me decades to learn that. And that there is pure evil in the world.

I also deal with severe depression and anxiety, and my daughter deals with this too. Dealing with these challenges, along with how Covid has changed our world, makes it difficult to concentrate and deal with life. My depression and feelings of being overwhelmed are debilitating at times, but I do my best — as we all do.

Positively, I experienced true love. I wasn't loved as a

child—my stepfather would use any opportunity to belittle me, abuse me mentally or physically, and, if my mother hugged or loved on me, he would "balance" it out with hurt and pain. I was sexually abused by his nephew and a first cousin on my mom's side.

Yes, I know. As adults, we are not supposed to talk about childhood abuse and trauma, definitely not in such detail. We're supposed to forgive, forget, and move on, to never talk about it again. I am here to change that stigma. But I do so to encourage those who are going through trauma, continuing to heal, and finding themselves and their purpose, as I still am.

I am older now and calling those people out for being horrible. I wasn't able to when I was younger. Now, I have a voice and a platform to do so.

My trauma allows me to write intimately and honestly about abuse. Just as finding someone who loved me through my pain and helped me heal, allowed me to believe in love. This is something that all the counseling in the world hadn't been able to help me do—hurdle the obstacle of feeling unlovable. Do not get me wrong. I appreciate all the therapy I've been blessed with, especially with Dr. Amy Berg in Portland, OR. Counseling set me up for healing when I did find love and someone who wouldn't give up on me. (I can't believe writing this brought me to tears.)

Love does conquer many of the trials we endure. Does it conquer all? Probably not. Love, too, is a choice. Not just any love, but true, unconditional love.

These are all the bits and pieces I needed to live through before this book series could come together. Before I could see Esmae, Simon, and the kismet books' magic and what it meant for them and for others before them. Yes, in this series the past loves the books connected and tried to connect will be revealed.

Life and love are wild journeys of choice and chance. The weaving of Esmae and Simon gets more entangled with positive and negative consequences. Because magic always has a price.

Keep reading as we find out together what happens on this journey.

To read a book is to open our minds
to the world of what is possible.
Whether learning about new worlds,
finding love, building relationships,
improving our lives, or having the
courage to stand up for our beliefs
and taking chances to change,
books empower us to be
the best version of ourselves.

What to Expect in:
The Book who Knew Me

In *The Book who Knew Me*, many aspects of Irish myths, legends, and fishing lore are integrated into the story. This research has taken more time then I realized it would. The way fishermen speak, the phrasing of stories, and the dry sense of Irish humor are intimate parts of what draws Esmae to Simon. They are both storytellers.

For many decades, Esmae has been a dutiful wife and mother. She's given selflessly and has no backbone, that's why she is indecisive. She doesn't know who she is without her family. Slowly, in *The Book who Knew* Me, this changes.

Simon has his own challenges to overcome to accept love again. We find out more about his story in the third book, *The Book who Loved Him*, which is about his life and journey to finding the book and why he wanted it.

Trust me, you will not be disappointed when it comes out. The connection between Esmae and Simon heats up. Of course, Simon doesn't know it is Esmae that he is writing to. He thinks it's the spirit of his dead wife or some magical Irish enchantment from an ancestral selkie.

Esmae knows the book is connecting her to someone special who is Irish, but beyond the words that are written, she has no idea who that someone is.

My vision was for three rapid release books for the first three parts in this Kismet Book series. That didn't happen for many reasons.

I am disappointed at not having the first three books in this series completed. Writing Esmae and Simon's journey, doing research, the plot development, and the emotional toll writing some scenes has taken, have all contributed to a delay in releasing them. I'm also working a full-time job and a single mom.

Thank you for understanding and your continued interest.

This kismet journey Esmae and Simon are on is exciting to me. I still don't know when they will end up together. They have many obstacles ahead of them, including an ocean. Esmae is scared to travel and Simon lost his wife at sea. I, too, wonder if they will be ready for a second chance at love at the same time.

Hang on to your Kindle or paperback as we see what happens. Thank you for going on this journey with Esmae, Simon, and me.

Look for *The Book who Knew Me* in a few months.

Find me on Instagram:
@sanz_edwards

Support the continued creation of this series on Patreon:
https://www.patreon.com/sanz_edwards

**If you or someone you know is dealing with
domestic abuse or violence, either call 911 or the
National Domestic Violence Hotline
1.800.799.SAFE (7233)
Or visit their website:
www.thehotline.org**

**If you or someone you know is
contemplating suicide, please call
National Suicide Prevention Lifeline
1.800.273.8255
Available 24 hours a day.
Or visit their website:
www.suicidepreventionlifeline.org**

Made in the USA
Monee, IL
24 April 2022